Cosy Christmas Treats

A collection of Christmas stories and feel-good tales by Choc Lit and Ruby Fiction authors

Where heroes are like chocolate – irresistible!

www.choc-lit.com

Stories that inspire emotions!

www.rubyfiction.com

Published 2020 by Choc Lit Publishing
Penrose House, Crawley Drive, Camberley, Surrey GU15 2AB, UK
www.choc-lit.com

A CIP catalogue record for this book is available from the British Library

EPUB ISBN: 978-1-78189-471-2

PRINT ISBN: 978-1-78189-469-9

Contents

Last Orders

Helen Bridgett

The jukebox pumped out 'White Christmas' and, as the customers started swaying in time to the music, it looked like a sea of rosy cheeks and pompoms had taken over the bar. Some of the more inebriated bellowed out the chorus and Peter watched them, shaking his head in amusement.

'Bing Crosby will be turning in his grave,' he murmured to himself. Sitting in a quiet corner of the pub and nursing a whisky, he looked up at the clock on the wall now framed in sparkly tinsel. 5.05 p.m., it would soon be time for the after-work throng to start piling in. His crowd would arrive at around quarter past; no earlier and no later. He wasn't really sure why he'd decided to get here before them but, just as well he had, as the place was really filling up; if he moved now, he could carve out a space at the bar.

Peter navigated the crowd wearing novelty jumpers as they swapped Secret Santa gifts. The mood was as cheerful as the lights twinkled on the huge Norwegian pine in the corner, and Peter knew he would stay here as long as he could tonight. There was no point leaving this festive warmth early, just to spend another Christmas alone. He reached the bar and tried to get the attention of the staff.

'That's the right thing to be drinking on a night like this,' said a sultry voice.

Peter turned to see an attractive young woman had perched herself on a stool next to him. 'I've always liked the thought of whisky, the golden colour and warm glow,' she continued circling her finger around the rim of her glass. 'But then when you have a sip, it just burns.'

'It's an acquired taste,' he agreed, delighted that she'd chosen to talk to him and wondering how on earth to keep this conversation going. He needn't have worried.

'Dreadful weather outside isn't it?' she continued. 'Just ghastly – I'd leave England for somewhere warmer if I could, wouldn't you?'

Peter nodded and said that he agreed with her; the weather was awful, they'd had the promise of snow for weeks but all that seemed to have arrived was horrible wet slush which soaked your shoes and chilled you to the bone. On finishing his sentence, he looked again at his new companion – from head to toe, she was completely bone dry so really couldn't have ventured out in that weather any time recently.

She was a very beautiful young woman and seemed vaguely familiar. Peter wondered whether she was an actress or one of those reality stars everyone else but him seemed to recognise. *In a station bar? Hardly likely.* She was staring at him now, seemingly inviting him to continue the conversation.

'I love your hair,' he said, digging for a compliment to pay her. 'That style really suits you.'

He had actually noticed her hair as soon as he'd looked at her. She wore an immaculate jet-black bob which seemed out of place amongst the storm-beaten tangles of the other women in the bar.

She nodded appreciatively. 'Thank you,' she replied. 'I'm Dorothy by the way.'

Peter thought it an unusual name for what he guessed was her age; all the twenty-somethings in his office were Aimees or Jasmines. But then everything about her was slightly *different.* Some women had it, he knew that; they could shop in a flea market and still come out looking immaculate. This woman wasn't even trying – no short hemlines, no revealing neckline and yet, in her quiet confidence, she exuded sexuality. He really was becoming more certain he'd seen her somewhere – but where?

‘Isn’t that delightfully ironic?’ said Dorothy, giggling and pointing to the mirror behind the bar.

He looked up at the fake Victoriana style mirror completed with etched graphics and elaborately swirling lettering. It was typical décor for this type of bar and not ironic at all as far as he could see.

‘Why?’ he asked.

‘*We serve a fine selection of spirits*,’ she read out, gazing up at him.

‘Still don’t get it,’ he replied.

‘Saying “we serve spirits” when they know the place is haunted,’ she explained, smiling at her own joke.

‘Surely you don’t believe in all that.’ Peter laughed. ‘Although if you have to haunt anywhere then it might as well be a pub!’

‘I don’t think you actually get a choice in the matter,’ replied Dorothy, her tone now softer and more contemplative. ‘I believe you have to haunt the place you passed.’

‘So did the poor soul who haunts this place die of food poisoning?’ joked Peter. ‘Now that wouldn’t surprise me at all.’

She smiled at him, the perfect red of her Clara Bow lips revealing even more perfect small white teeth.

‘Can I buy you a drink?’ asked Peter, feeling a strong wave of affection for this stranger.

She shook her head. ‘I still have this one and I can’t have you getting me tipsy.’ She held her martini glass elegantly between two gloved fingers. He hadn’t seen her take a sip, but he’d been nursing his whisky for just as long so perhaps both of them were taking it easy – not like last night.

‘Is that your crowd over there?’ she asked.

Peter looked over at the entrance and, sure enough, on the dot of 5.15, his colleagues walked in, ties loosened and top buttons undone, ready to relax. They looked particularly downbeat as they pushed their way through to the bar and Peter guessed they were all really ready for this break. The group walked up to the far end of the bar and started ordering drinks. Peter knew he should get up and join them but didn’t want to leave his new companion. There was something about her; it wasn’t a lightning bolt of passion he felt. It was something calmer, more peaceful. Peter wanted to take his time with Dorothy.

‘You need to go,’ she said suddenly, making the decision for him and standing up.

‘I don’t have to,’ said Peter, hoping he didn’t sound desperate. ‘I’ll tell them that I’ve met someone, they’ll understand.’

‘No, really,’ replied Dorothy placing a hand gently on his arm. ‘You have to go.’

‘But … can I see you again?’ stuttered Peter. ‘I mean, do you come here often, if that’s not too corny a question?’

Dorothy smiled. ‘Oh yes, ‘I’m always here.’ And with that, she took a step backwards and faded into the wall.

Peter stood, dumbfounded. He looked around to see if anyone else had witnessed it, but the crowd was still singing and swaying as if nothing had happened.

‘Woah,’ he said under his breath. ‘She was talking about herself.’

Still unsteady, he stumbled his way towards his friends. Should he tell them about this? Frankly, it sounded ridiculous. ‘Guys – I’ve just been chatted up by a gorgeous ghost,’ he practised as he walked.

When he reached his friends, their conversation was in full flow. Peter tried to interrupt. ‘You’re never going to guess what’s just happened …’ he started.

His workmates fell silent and then John, his boss, raised his glass.

‘To Peter,’ he said with an affectionate smile on his face.

Before Peter could interject, the rest of the team raised their glasses.

‘To absent friends,’ they said.

‘Absent? I’m here you idiots,’ shouted Peter but no-one turned to him.

And then it came; the blinding light, the violent flashback to last night. He’d been in here, he’d had a few too many. He’d watched all the couples snuggling up together and determined that he wasn’t going to spend another Christmas alone. He’d drunkenly tried to kiss some strangers under the mistletoe, but they’d pushed him off. He’d staggered outside onto the street then saw her, on the opposite side of the road – a beautiful woman with jet-black hair and full red lips. She’d smiled and beckoned to him.

‘Why on earth would he run across the road?’ asked one of his friends.

‘They say that bus had no chance of stopping,’ said another before shivering and adding. ‘It’s blooming freezing in here tonight.’

Peter looked down at the ghostly mist shrouding his body and realised *he* was that cold chill. He wanted to cry out, but it would do no good. Dorothy re-appeared and held out her hand to him. Peter walked towards her, the crowd neither acknowledging nor hindering his path.

'It was you,' he said. 'Why?'

'I hate being alone too, especially at Christmas,' replied Dorothy. 'And it's not so bad here. After all, they do serve a fine selection of spirits.'

* The End *

Find out more about Helen Bridgett and her novels here: https://www.rubyfiction.com/productcat/helen-bridgett/

Helen's novels include: *Summer at Serenity Bay* & *One by One*

Lily McKee's Seven Days of Christmas

Chris Penhall

December 19th

'Your new job is very impressive, but I'm not at all happy with it at the moment.'

Lily listened to the voicemail for the third time just to hear her mother's voice. And, of course, she was right. A new job, a new start, a new flat, a new town. More money, more prospects, more everything. It was indeed impressive. But the huge and obvious downside was that Lily would be completely on her own for Christmas – for the first time in her life.

'Why do you have to live so far away?' she muttered at the phone. 'Yes, I know. Rhetorical question.'

Her family had lived in Canada for years. It was Lily who had decided to move back to the UK when she was twenty-two to have an adventure. And it was a great adventure. It really was. But every Christmas for the past nine years, she'd flown back to visit the clan in Montreal. She had always somehow managed to book a full two weeks off, as had her wonderful and faithful long-term boyfriend, Jeff.

Not this year. She was six months single. Jeff had decided that he didn't want to be faithful anymore and needed an adventure before he hit forty – which was still eight years off. So, he'd given up his job in international banking, followed a free spirit called Fleur to Fuerteventura and started teaching in a surfing school. He liked the idea of the sand dunes, apparently.

Lily was pursuing her own dreams – although, they weren't quite so life-changing – and had been appointed area director of the company she was already working for. This was why she had moved to an unfamiliar place three weeks before Christmas and why, as the new girl, she had to work right up to Christmas Eve. Then, after a three-day break – which would be alone, alone, all alone – back to her job on December 27th.

Lily looked at the calendar hanging on the wall which showed it was December 19th. Then she glanced around the tidy, warm, welcoming flat, completely devoid of festive spirit, took a pen and scratched through "Go to see the family at Christmas". *Yay!* she thought, grimly. Then she wrote "Get Christmas decorations" on December 20th. That was the date when her family in Canada did it. They always waited until she arrived so they could all dress the tree together. 'It will be fine,' she said to Lola the cat, who was waiting patiently at her feet for some treats.

A clatter on the path outside interrupted her thoughts and she peered out of the window. A removal van had parked up, and two men were unsteadily carrying a large piece of, what looked like, electrical equipment along next door's front path, whilst another man was picking up some metal poles from the pavement.

'Be careful,' he said loudly as they disappeared towards the back garden. 'My pride and joy. Need it for my Christmas project.'

'Did you say you wanted it in the shed?' shouted one of the men.

'It's a workshop. And yes.' He stood up and turned around, giving Lily an opportunity to study her new neighbour. He was tall, he was good-looking, and he was wearing a jumper with a snowman on the front.

'Happy Christmas to me,' she muttered, as he absent-mindedly scratched his face. 'Very Idris Elba.' Then she moved away quickly as he looked up to the window. She didn't want to appear nosy. She wasn't, she told herself, she was merely curious.

‘Probably married. Or has a partner. They always do,’ she muttered to Lola, who had jumped up onto the sofa and was now stretching along it proprietorially. ‘Are you going to make any room for me?’ The cat rolled over and closed her eyes. ‘That’s a no, then.’

Putting on the kettle, Lily made a cup of chamomile tea, turned on her computer and got back to work, trying to block out the bangs and shouts coming from outside.

December 20th

Lily picked up the card attached to the huge parcel that had been delivered that morning. It was wrapped in red, shiny paper and topped off with a massive cream bow. It said, *As you can’t get to your traditional Christmas wardrobe we keep for you over here, we’ve sent another one to you, so you can count the days down as if you were with us. Mum, Dad and the fam xx xxx*. Lily smiled, then tore the bow and paper off it like she used to when she was an excited little girl. Inside were red, green, gold, silver and black dresses, traditional Christmas jumpers and various headbands, reindeer antlers and bauble earrings.

Picking up a snowman bracelet, she let herself have a cry – she'd be wearing it alone this year, after all – then took a deep breath, calmed herself down and picked out a green woollen dress to wear to the garden centre.

All the trees looked the same to her, but the one thing she knew was important was that her very first Christmas tree – the first one she would ever buy for herself – had to be small enough to carry home on foot, but big enough to give a sense of occasion when she got there.

Eventually she stopped trying to compare the trees like her parents did. *How did they spend so much time talking about them, discussing the merits of each, then arguing, and finally agreeing on exactly the same one?* She decided that maybe she had a Christmas tree choosing gene missing and took the easy route, which meant closing her eyes, pointing randomly, and opening her eyes again. *Very scientific*, she thought, *but you it is – you are my tree*. She waved at the assistant. 'I'll take this one please.'

She realised she hadn't thought the process through properly around ten minutes into the walk home, as dragging a large conifer along a damp pavement turned out to be hard work.

By the time Lily got to the corner of her street, she was decidedly sweaty, her hair frizzed in the damp winter air, and her nose red with the cold. She paused for a moment, taking a breath to prepare for the last 100 metres stretch, then bent down to grab the tree again, somehow getting her scarf caught in the netting. 'Oh, no,' she sighed, trying to pull it off, but managing to get it even more tangled. In the end, she gave up and attempted to take the scarf off, but got the other end stuck too. Gritting her teeth, she let out an inward scream, then pulled the tree up to her shoulders and trudged on, but this time pulling it backwards.

A car stopped just ahead of her

'Do you need any help there?' It was her new neighbour.

Lily could feel her face go as red as her coat. 'Oh, yes please … this seemed like such a good idea when I started out.'

He got out of the car. 'How much further have you got to go?'

'I live at number 29.'

'Oh, hello number 29. I've just moved in next door. I'm Jason … or your knight in shining armour.' He laughed.

Lily gazed up at him, flustered. His eyes crinkled attractively as he smiled. 'Lily,' she said. 'Nice to meet you, Jason Knight in Shining Armour.'

'Shall I?' He picked up the other end of the tree as if it was as light as a feather and helped Lily carry it to her front door. 'Do you need any help unravelling the scarf?' he asked, once she had managed to get her key in the lock.

'No, that's fine, but thank you,' she said. What she actually thought was, *No... I'm a grown woman tangled up in my own scarf and attached to a Christmas tree. I want to turn the clock back and reappear as an attractive career woman in control of my life, having my tree delivered by a Harrods van at the same time as a hamper from Fortnum and Mason.*

'Right then.' He looked into her eyes again. 'Well, best get on. Nice to meet you Lily.'

'Nice to meet you too.'

He waved from the end of the path as Lily backed into the house, dragging the Christmas tree behind her. Then she closed the door and slid to the floor before taking another twenty minutes to disentangle herself.

She made herself a mug of hot chocolate and sat on the window seat in her bedroom, watching the Christmas lights sparkle in the surrounding houses. *The Saturday night before Christmas*, she thought, *with nowhere to go*. Standing up, she shook her new snow globe, covering a reindeer and Santa Claus in tiny shimmering flakes. It reminded her of evenings spent watching the world turn slowly white as the snow fluttered onto the garden and the fields and the mountains at home.

Turning back to the window, she saw a green flash and heard a sudden loud bang coming from the workshop at the bottom of Jason's garden. Then suddenly all his house lights went out, shrouding everything in darkness.

Lily leaned forward and peered outside, wondering whether to go and check that he was alright, then saw him hurry out and along the path to the side of his house. Two minutes later, she heard a knock on the door and went downstairs, forgetting she was wearing a headband covered in flashing baubles.

She straightened her green wool dress – chosen to match the tree – and opened the door.

'Hi.' Jason looked a little sheepish. 'Do you have a torch at all? I've blown all the lights and need to find the fuse box. It's too dark to find my own.' Then he laughed. 'Although I could use you and your headband.'

Lily felt her hair. 'Oh gosh, I forgot about that,' she said, walking to the kitchen. 'Do come in. I heard a noise and was wondering if you were alright.'

'I'm fine,' he said, following her in. 'Me blowing fuses when I'm working on my projects is not unusual.'

Lily found the torch in a drawer and handed it to him. 'What are you working on?'

'Oh, just something for Christmas,' he said, vaguely. 'Thanks for this.'

'Do you need any help?' Lily had no idea what she could possibly do but felt she ought to offer. He did have a very, *very* kind face, and she wanted to look at it for a while longer.

'Thanks. But I've still got loads to unpack and I think the house is a bit of a hazard. Maybe another time.' He flashed her a smile and left. She felt her stomach filling with little butterflies dancing around excitedly as she watched him hurry down the path.

She walked upstairs to retrieve her mug and, as she took it off the windowsill, the workshop began to glow green and she wondered what he could possibly have at the bottom of the garden that was such a strange and luminous colour.

December 21st

Lily put her headphones on and closed the front door behind her, having decided a jog in the park would take her mind off the prospect of spending Christmas Day alone. Well, it would take her mind off it for an hour, and an hour was better than nothing. She clicked on her festive playlist, but just as Slade began to blast out of the headphones, the sound of banging and crashing from the vicinity of Jason's house drowned out the music. She stood for a moment, wondering once again whether checking up on him was a good idea, then thought better of it, and headed off for her exercise.

Jason was in his front garden when Lily arrived back, kneeling next to several pieces of wood.

'Hello.' She waved. 'Still working on your project?'

'Yes. Got a deadline.' He flashed that smile again. 'I like the tinsel on your headphones.'

Lily laughed. 'Ah yes. I like to make a festive effort you know. Normally I'm with my family in Montreal by now, so this year I'm trying even harder to have a sense of occasion in virtually everything I do.'

'Well, it's very fetching.' He held her gaze for a moment, but then his phone rang. 'Sorry, got to get this.'

'Bye then.' Lily went back into her house and wondered how to keep herself occupied until she went to bed. In the end, she booked herself a seat at the local cinema for a special showing of *Elf*, moved the tinsel from her headphones to her coat, and headed off into the dark winter's night.

December 22nd

Lily opened the curtains to frost glittering on the grass and glowing in the trees. Later on, her family would wake up thousands of miles away, excited for their annual moonlight open air ice skating session and hot toddies, whereas Lily anticipated a day at work, followed by a trip to the supermarket to buy a turkey.

Pulling on her dressing-gown, she noticed a red glow, then orange flashes, coming from Jason's shed. She was about to turn away but he opened the door and sat on the step, then looked up and noticed her watching – Lily told herself she was merely glancing – and he waved, flashing that smile again. Lily waved back, his unshaven face sending the butterflies in her stomach into a frenzy.

What earth was he doing in there? she wondered, taking her red jersey dress decorated with white flecks out of the wardrobe. The woollen version with the white fluffy tassels attached to virtually everything hung tantalisingly in front of her. 'Not today, lovely dress,' she said. 'Not to work.' Then she treated herself to another quick glance at Jason, who was now doing press-ups on the decking, and flung herself into the shower.

The supermarket was heaving with last minute festive shoppers and, try as she might, Lily was unable to resist a set of pink fairy lights in the shape of Tinkerbells that reminded her of the ones her parents had on their tree. As soon as she saw them, she grabbed them and held them tight, as if they'd make her feel closer to her family. But they didn't. At that moment, as other people's families pushing trollies laden with Christmas goods swirled around her, she felt a very long way from them indeed. She grabbed an extra bottle of Prosecco, tried not to cry in the queue – because a thirty-one-year-old woman in tears over fairy lights was a difficult one to explain – and rushed home.

Jason was in full flow with his mysterious project and, as she unpacked her shopping, Lily felt strangely comforted with the noise of the hammering and drilling drifting over the garden fence. Storing the Prosecco in the freezer to speed up the chilling process, she decorated her already well-dressed Christmas tree with her new lights and plugged them in.

Then everything went black.

'Oh, no …' Lily muttered, leaning against the wall and sliding down into a helpless mess on the floor, finally allowing the tears to trickle down her face. Home seemed even further away than it had in the supermarket.

Pulling herself together, she stood up, straightened her dress and dried her eyes, then began to rifle through the kitchen drawers for her torch, just as someone knocked on the door.

'Hi … Lily. It's me, Jason. I think you may need your torch. And I have it.'

The butterflies surged excitedly. *Every cloud*, she thought as she let him in.

'New fairy lights.' She pointed in the direction of the living room. 'Took the whole house out.'

'Took mine out, too.' He smiled. 'But I know where the fuse box is now … there must be some kind of glitch that connects the houses. I'll check it out another time.'

'At the risk of sounding a bit pathetic, I've only been in here a few weeks myself and haven't located the fuse box yet. Because I haven't had to.'

'Follow me,' he said. Then he turned back to her. 'You do have a cupboard under the stairs, don't you?'

'Yes. Here.' Lily fumbled around – it really was pitch black – and opened the door.

'Okay. I'm going in, since I have the torch. There's nothing breakable in there, is there?'

'No, I'm all unpacked,' she said, watching Jason feel his way in along the wall. The lights came on as suddenly as they'd gone off, and Lily and Jason found themselves standing very close together.

'Thank you,' she said.

'You're welcome.' He grinned down at her. 'I like your dress. You're very festive.'

'Well, I try.' Lily hesitated for a moment, to let the butterflies calm down. 'I've got some Prosecco chilling … would you like a glass as a thank you?'

Jason checked his watch, then nodded. 'Yes, okay. Just a quick one … I've got this deadline, you see, but I could do with a break.'

Lily retrieved the bottle from the freezer. 'I was fast tracking it,' she said.

'To make time from purchase to chilling to drinking speedier?' He laughed.

'Absolutely.'

She took out some festive glasses decorated with gold filigree and poured them both a drink.

'So, what is this project?' she asked. 'You seem to be working on it all the time.'

'Ah, well. I'm a lighting engineer on films and events and a bit of a space nerd so ...' His phone pinged and he checked the message. 'Sorry, again … it's to do with the project. What about you Lily? Have you been here long?'

'In the house a month. At my new job for three weeks. I go to Canada every Christmas normally, to visit my family, so this is a bit unusual for me. Hence the festive dresses and loads of decorations. That's what my family do, so I'm just replicating it, I suppose.'

'So, are you going to friends on Christmas Day?'

‘No. I’m riding it out alone. It’s all rather last minute. It’ll be fine.’ That was the first time Lily had ever thought about Christmas as something she needed to get through rather than look forward to. She took a sip of her Prosecco and tried not to feel sad.

‘Oh, that’s ...’ Jason’s phone pinged again. ‘I’ve got to go. Delivery arriving.’ He finished his drink quickly. ‘Thank you,’ he said. ‘And I won’t steal your torch this time.’ He smiled again and rushed out of the door.

Lily felt the butterflies in her stomach dance as she watched him go and poured herself another glass of Prosecco.

December 23rd

Lily wore her silver top and black sparkly leggings to the work festive lunch, topped by a headband adorned with tiny polar bears wearing red-striped jumpers. It made her question her mother’s sanity – I mean, where had she found it? – but it also made her smile all day.

She meandered home, enjoying the cold, crisp December air. Snippets of Christmas songs spilled out of shops, and she stopped for a few moments to listen to a group of carol singers performing under the town's Christmas tree. Further ahead, the smell of roasting chestnuts drew her in to a pop-up farmers' market, and she bought herself some cake and pâte to take home, planning a night of back to back films – *Miracle on 34th Street*, *The Holiday* and maybe *Home Alone* if she had time. She was saving *Love Actually* till Christmas Eve, and *It's a Wonderful Life* till Christmas Day.

Her family would be at their traditional Christmas carol sing-along festival that evening, after popping into see their neighbours Barb and Phil for the annual highly alcoholic Eggnog Meet and Greet. They would all be wearing their Christmas jumpers and matching bright red bobble hats. She missed them again. It washed over her like a wave, then subsided as she saw Jason waving at her from the mulled wine stall.

'I'm having a break,' he said. 'Suddenly realised I didn't have anything Christmassy in at all. Well, I've got a delivery coming, but I do like some extra bits and pieces, you know.'

'I've never made a Christmas dinner before. I think I've overbought.'

'I have too. I'll be able to live off this particular shop for about six weeks!' He laughed and handed her a glass. 'Happy Christmas.' He smiled. 'That headband is very impressive.'

'A gift from my mother. She managed to source it from somewhere.'

'Are you missing your family? It can't be nice being away from them at this time of year.'

'Yes I am.' Lily took a sip of the wine. 'But it's only a few days, isn't it? I'll make the best of it, and next year will be back to normal. I hope.'

Jason looked serious for a moment, then gazed down at her. 'If you're—' But he was suddenly interrupted when a large man carrying two small children shouted 'Jason!' at him, then waved. 'Mate … how've you been?'

'I'm—'

'Sorry, can't manage to move. Can you come over here? I need to talk to you about tomorrow.'

Jason looked at Lily and shrugged. 'Sorry. Again. I have to go. It's about the—'

'Project.' Lily laughed. 'It's fine. Thank you for the mulled wine. I'd best be off anyway.'

He put his arm on her shoulder as if he was about to say something just as one of the children started to cry. He looked over at his friend and sighed. 'I'd best go.'

She watched him greet the group, letting the little butterflies skip around in her stomach a bit more, then walked back to her empty house. She switched on her fairy lights, cut herself a piece of cake, put on her Christmas socks and smiled to herself when she heard Jason arrive home and restart his colourful DIY on his mysterious project.

December 24th

Christmas Eve dawned, the sky a clear, cold blue, brightening up the kitchen as Lily took her speciality festive cookies out of the oven. This was another family tradition, and she planned to send them the photographs later to show how gorgeous they were, although a picture could not convey the wonderful gingerbread smell filling the kitchen. 'Santa Claus is Coming to Town' was blasting out of the radio and Lola sat on the windowsill, watching Lily jig around in her Rudolph Christmas jumper and Santa hat. Lily felt almost content. *Only got to get through tomorrow*, she thought. *Then my first Christmas alone will be done*.

Something banged and fizzed in Jason's shed. Lily nibbled on one of the biscuits and wondered if he needed some sustenance. 'Why not?' she said to herself, placing a few cookies on a plate. 'I'm just being neighbourly.'

Lily adjusted her hat and knocked on the workshop door. 'Jason,' she shouted over the drilling. 'Jason.' The noise stopped and she knocked again.

The door opened and there he stood, looking a bit beardy and messy and very, *very* attractive. Lily's butterflies went mad.

'Home-made cookies,' she said, holding out the plate. 'I've made rather a lot and I wondered if you'd like some.'

He smiled, his eyes crinkling. 'Thank you.' He looked behind him. 'I'd invite you in, but I'm almost done and at a bit of a critical point.'

'Oooh, biscuits,' said a woman's voice out of the darkness. 'I could do with something to eat.'

A tall, smiley lady appeared and stood next to him. 'Hi. I'm Alison. They smell delicious. Did you make these?'

The butterflies plummeted to the pit of Lily's stomach and stayed there. 'Yes. I just made quite a lot.' She stepped back. 'I'm Lily. I live next door … I'd best be off. You look very busy.'

‘We’ve got to get it finished by four. Well, Jason has. I’ve got to rush off to work in a mo. Thanks for the biscuits.’

‘Hopefully see you later. Like the jumper.’ Jason smiled. ‘I’ve got to go. Deadline. As usual.’ He shrugged apologetically and Lily backed down the path as he closed the door, muttering ‘I’m a cliché,’ as she got back to her house. She spent the afternoon under a duvet watching *Love Actually*.

When she eventually climbed out of her little hideaway, Lily made herself a cup of tea and watched the lights next door spill out of the workshop, green and yellow and orange and pink, accompanied by David Bowie singing ‘Star Man’, then heard the tune to ‘Northern Lights’. She smiled, despite her gloom, and climbed the stairs to get the Christmas presents her parents had sent so she could put them under the tree.

Looking out of the bedroom window, she saw that Jason’s garden was full of people, with adults and children queuing to get into the workshop. Groups were standing around drinking mulled wine and chatting, as the lights inside the workshop glowed and shone, accompanied by music, applause and cheers.

'What is that?' she asked the cat who was sitting watching, mesmerised by the lights. 'No, I've got no idea either, Lola.'

As she carried the presents downstairs, someone rang the doorbell. Lily put them on the floor, adjusted her Santa hat and opened the door.

'Hi, Lily. It's Alison. From next door … the one who took all the biscuits.'

'Oh, hello, Alison. I hope you enjoyed them.'

'Delicious. Thank you again. I thought you may like to come and see what Jason's made, seeing as the noise must be disrupting your evening.'

A school mini-bus slid into a parking space in front of the house, joining several others along the road. Lily watched, surprised and confused. The running time of *Love Actually* was only two hours and twenty-five minutes, so when had all these people arrived? 'It's no disruption,' she said. 'But I am intrigued.'

'Follow me. I'll fast track you.' Alison laughed, taking Lily's arm and guiding her through the people. 'Jason … Jason!' she shouted from the doorway. 'Why don't you go in?' She smiled. 'I've got to get my lot back to the hospital. They're the siblings of some of the children who are having to stay in over

Christmas. It's a bit of a treat for them and their parents.'

She pushed Lily gently inside.

Lily looked up as the darkness began to light up with stars and meteors, as if they were flying above her, then the sun rose and set, giving way to a big orange moon. Suddenly, the lights went off again and the room was filled with green lights, and flashes of blue and pink and orange, the music soaring in the background. A hand took hers, and the butterflies skipped and fluttered excitedly.

'Did my bossy sister shove you in here?' he whispered.

'Alison? Your sister?' The butterflies went into overdrive. 'Yes, she did.'

'This is my project,' he said proudly, waving his arms around.

'It's beautiful.' Lily looked up at him, puzzled. 'What is it exactly?'

'A representation of the night sky and, of course, my very favourite, the northern lights.' He bowed. 'I am the ultimate astronomy stroke engineer stroke lighting professional nerd. I do this every year for some of the less fortunate children in the area as a

Christmas treat. But, as I've only just moved in here, it was a bit of a tight schedule.'

'It's beautiful,' sighed Lily. 'And what a lovely thing to do.' She felt as if the butterflies were applauding or cheering or just jumping up and down.

'I was hoping for a nice sprinkling of snow today, to add that extra festive touch, but my expertise doesn't extend to controlling the weather.' He squeezed her hand just as a group of children burst in, laughing excitedly.

'I'd better go,' he said. 'Duty calls.' He looked as if he was about to say something else, but simply smiled and went back to the control desk.

Lily walked out into the garden and floated home, just as her mobile phone rang.

'Hi, Mum. Hi, Dad,' she squealed. 'Happy Christmas Eve … no, I'm not at a party … it's more … my neighbour's made the northern lights in his shed … I mean workshop … and … well, it's difficult to explain … but I'm good. How are you all in Montreal?'

Lily sat, drinking Prosecco and eating chocolates, watching *The Muppet Christmas Carol*. Another family tradition. As the credits rolled, she heard a knock at the door.

Jason stood on the step, snow falling softly around him. He had a Santa hat on his head, a red flashing bow tie around his neck and a bottle of wine in his hand.

'I managed to get the snow to work,' he said, then laughed. 'Well, the weather changed, but I'll take credit for it. Wondered if you felt like some company, seeing as we're both home alone for Christmas?'

Lily flung the door open wide. 'Do come in.' The butterflies almost sang.

'It's just me and Alison usually, and this year she is working. So …'

'I was actually planning on watching *Home Alone*. I saved it from yesterday.'

'Well, that's us. I hope you don't think I'm too pushy or forward or anything. It's just …'

Lily stepped closer. 'Just what?'

'When I saw you dragging your Christmas tree along the road ...'

'Yes ...'

'I think I felt butterflies in my stomach. I'm a grown man. Butterflies!'

'Butterflies?'

‘And every time I saw you in a Christmas dress or a Christmas jumper or with a funny headband … they came back.’ He stepped closer. ‘I found it difficult to concentrate on my project, to be honest.’

‘I think your project is wonderful,’ Lily whispered.

He took some mistletoe out of his pocket and held it over her head. ‘You never know when you’re going to need some,’ he said, kissing her softly, then pulling him to her and kissing her some more.

December 25th

‘Happy Christmas, Lily.’

‘Happy Christmas, Jason.’

‘Shall I?’

‘Yes please.’

He flicked the switch, and the northern lights swirled around them, flakes of snow outside fluttering down and landing softly on the windows.

‘I’ve never spent Christmas Day in a shed before.’ Lily laughed.

‘Workshop,’ said Jason. ‘I like your Christmas dress.’

Lily smoothed the sleeves of the red dress and adjusted a white fluffy tassel. ‘I like your Christmas jumper.’

‘I always wear my Rudolph jumper on Christmas Day.’

‘I feel like I’m in a snow globe,’ she sighed, putting her arms around him. ‘This is perfect.’

He reached across and grabbed a bottle of champagne that was next to her on the floor. ‘Festive drink?’

‘Please.’ Lily smiled, thinking her very first Christmas alone was not too bad. *Not too bad at all.*

** The End **

Find out more about Chris Penhall and her novels here: https://www.rubyfiction.com/productcat/chris-penhall/

Chris’s novels include: New Beginnings at the Little House in the Sun & The House That Alice Built.

When Santa Calls

Jan Baynham

'Isn't it about time we bought a tree, Kathy?'

I looked at Steve and knew I should be making more of an effort.

'We could go this afternoon, if you like.' I tried to make my voice as cheery as possible, but nothing could disguise the fact that my heart just wasn't in it this year. Every time I'd ventured out of the house lately, I was reminded that the festive season was in full swing … but without *me*. The shops had been full of gaudy colour and glittery decorations for months and if I heard another rendition of 'Jingle Bells', I'd scream. What had happened to the true meaning of Christmas? Why did everything have to be so showy and over the top?

The garden centre was overflowing with everything Christmassy: shiny baubles, twinkling lights and festive garlands. We hadn't been to this one before. *Let's try a new one for a change,* I'd insisted. We found our way to the back where rows upon rows of fir trees were displayed.

'This one's a nice shape,' Steve said. 'What do you think?'

‘Yes, it's fine. You choose.’ I looked over my husband and realised he was making an effort, just for me. His eyes revealed what he really felt. They lacked the sparkle they normally showed when the fun of decorating the house started.

‘I think Alex would approve, don't you?’ he said.

Steve forced a grin as he held up a large evenly shaped tree for me to see. It was always something the three of us did together every year. *But not this year,* I thought. I could feel tears pricking along my eyelids and moved away so that Steve wouldn't see. *This is ridiculous*, I told myself. *What about all the other people whose loved ones will* never *be coming for Christmas again? It’s only one year, for goodness sake.* I remembered how Alex would run up and down the aisles shouting, ‘This one’. Once we got to him and his chosen tree, he’d run on to the next and then say, ‘No, this one’. He repeated his little game again and again, laughing each time. We were both daft enough to indulge him and it became our tradition every year. We were lucky that they knew us so well at our local garden centre and they allowed us our little ritual as long as it wasn’t too busy.

Christmas was always a family time for us. It took on a new magical meaning once Alex had come along after so many years of thinking we'd never have children. All the secrets we kept to prolong the wonder of Santa for as long as we could came flooding back. I smiled when I thought of the Christmas Eve rituals of putting out mince pies and milk, carrots for Rudolph and sprinkling sparkly reindeer food in the grass, hanging up Alex's stocking and creeping upstairs late at night to fill it. Even when he got older, we had surprise presents. No one knew until Christmas morning what to expect.

The tree did get decorated. The pale blue musical bauble with '*Special Boy's 1st Christmas*' took pride of place as always. Steve and I did it together and once he switched on the fairy lights, I began to feel better. Perhaps it wouldn't be so bad after all. The outside lights would be the talk of the street as always and we laughed together how friends would turn up their noses as they did every year at the twinkling icicles and nodding reindeer on the lawn. We stood outside in the cul-de-sac to admire this year's efforts.

'Hmm. Not our thing, I'm afraid, old man,' said Steve, mimicking our friend Dave in his best BBC voice.

'I presume you're trying to outdo the blinking Griswolds again,' I said, taking off our neighbour,

Wyn, who reluctantly managed a few tasteful white lights in his hallway after a lot of nagging from his wife.

Tacky it might be, but it was our family joke. Steve put his arm around my shoulders and pulled me close.

'Alex would love it, wouldn't he?' I said, my voice cracking.

'Yes, love, I think he would.' It was Steve's turn to move away and we went back into the house.

It was dark outside by then and everywhere was lit up. The house was displayed with its usual array of Christmas ornaments and it did look festive, I had to admit that. If Alex was going to be on Facetime from the heat of the Adelaide sun, we'd better make it look like the traditional Christmases past for him to show to his new Australian girlfriend.

The forecast had promised a white Christmas and sure enough, it started to snow as if on cue as Steve and I opened our presents on Christmas morning. Soon everything was glistening like silver in the low winter sun. *A traditional Christmas card scene.*

'All we need now is Santa to arrive on his sleigh in this snow,' said Steve.

‘Do you know this is the first white Christmas since goodness knows when and we forgot to leave out carrots for Rudolph and his friends last night?’ I said, laughing. ‘He won’t call here.’

‘You never know.’

It seemed strange cooking Christmas dinner for just the two of us. Steve did appear to have forgotten, though, judging by the amount of vegetables he’d prepared. *Bubble and squeak for days afterwards, then,* I thought, smiling. And to think he’d suggested we go out to a restaurant this year.

‘Just think, love. No preparation, no washing up, no hassle,’ he’d said.

But it didn’t seem right somehow. Anyway, I wanted to be there when Alex Facetimed us. I was up to my elbows washing the pans that wouldn’t fit in the dishwasher.

‘Are you *sure* you wouldn’t have preferred to go out for Christmas?’ he said, teasing.

I laughed and flicked some soap suds at him. I dried my hands and poured out some more Buck’s Fizz. Perhaps Christmas Day was going to be a good one after all.

Everything was nearly ready. The table was laid out with the best china and crystal glasses. We were just waiting for the dreaded sprouts to soften a little and then we could dish out. A little voice rang in my ear. '*Why do we always have to have sprouts, Mum, just because it's Christmas?*' How Alex had hated sprouts when he was little, but he'd always tried a little bit "just for Santa".

The doorbell rang.

'Can you answer it, love? I'll go and check on the dinner.' Steve went back into the kitchen.

'Whoever can this be calling on Christmas Day?' I said.

I opened the door and blinked as the strong sunlight blinded me. I raised my hand to shield my eyes; there was no one there.

'Ta dah!'

From the side of the house jumped a tall, hooded figure of Santa Claus, dressed head to toe in plush red velour, with just his eyes showing above a full, snowy white beard. I didn't recognise him at first, but then he held out his arms.

'G'day. Your very own Secret Santa all the way from Oz! Happy Christmas, Mum.'

'Alex!'

By this time, Steve was by my side. ‘Didn’t I say that Santa may call?’

‘And here’s my beautiful helper,’ said Alex. A beaming girl with long blonde hair came and stood by him. ‘Mum, Dad. This is Maddie, and she can’t wait to try your famous sprouts!’

** The End **

Christmas Surprises on Péfka

Jan Baynham

Alexandra pulled open the bi-fold doors running the full length of the living room. It was the first time in weeks she'd been able to do so. Drinking in the panoramic view of the sea, she breathed in crisp December air. During the intense heat of the summer months, she'd never have imagined the island she now called home would have wet weather like they'd be having back in Wales. But today, there wasn't a cloud in the sky and the sun was out at last. The sea had returned to its beautiful shade of aquamarine and, in the distance, sugar lump houses on the mainland glistened once again.

Her throat constricted and tears burned along her eyelids. It took her by surprise. It didn't make sense. Her pottery business had been up and running for over six months now. It was doing well. In fact, with the build-up to Christmas, she was busier than ever. Although Christmas wasn't viewed with the same significance as Easter here on the Greek island, there had definitely been an upturn in the number of commission orders she'd been getting. Her plates and bowls in sea colours, with semi-matte glazes in muted shades of turquoise and teal, were not only displayed here in her studio but down in the shops skirting the harbour as well.

Pull yourself together, cariad. Her mam's voice with its gentle Welsh lilt entered her head, making her gasp. Yes, that was it. It was the first Christmas she'd be spending away from her nan and her sister, Claire. That was why she felt the way she did. But she'd made her home with her Greek family on this beautiful island now. It had been her decision. Mam was right.

After closing the doors, Alexandra went into the studio at the back of the one-storey building. She checked that the slabs of clay she'd rolled out earlier were dry enough for her to carve and cut out the Christmas decorations she'd planned to sell in the studio shop. The new lustre glazes would be arriving from Ermioni soon, and excitement at the prospect of opening up the kiln to reveal silver snowflakes, golden angels and bells fizzled through her. The melancholy retreated. *Everything would be fine*, she told herself, and Claire would ensure her grandmother had a lovely Christmas.

Yiannis sat waiting at their usual table in Xante's taverna. Since the weather had become cooler, instead of sitting outside under the bright blue parasols, they now sat by the large picture windows overlooking the harbour. He stood as Alexandra entered and beamed. He kissed her on both cheeks; the hint of musky aftershave caused her stomach to somersault.

'Sorry I'm a bit late,' she said. 'I just wanted to get the last lot of snowflakes done so they can dry out enough for tomorrow's firing.'

'Snowflakes will be a novelty here on Péfka, I think, eh?'

Alexandra smiled at her boyfriend. 'Well, you said there wouldn't be Christmas trees here like we have in Wales, but I counted at least seven on the way down the hill from my place. There are nearly three weeks to go yet. I'm sure people will love them once they're glazed, all sparkly and catching the lights.'

'What I mean is, *agápi mou*, is that most of them haven't seen real snow here for many winters.' Yiannis took Alexandra's hand and stroked her fingers. 'By the feel of it, I'm sure these hands will create beautiful decorations for the Christmas trees on Péfka. Come on, let's eat. I've ordered some raki to warm us whilst we choose.'

Alexandra sipped the clear spirit and let the burn travel through her as she studied the menu. She knew what she'd be having without having to look, and Yiannis went up to the bar to order. When she'd arrived on the island eighteen months before, she would never have believed that, not only would she have found her Greek father, Stelios, but fallen in love, too. She remembered how, armed with her mother's diary, she'd followed in her footsteps to find out what happened to her mother in the eventful summer of 1969. And here she was with her own pottery business and a beautiful home courtesy of a Greek father who was making up for the twenty years he hadn't known she'd existed.

The handsome young man sitting opposite her had helped her find her father and they were now inseparable. She couldn't imagine life without Yiannis but told herself she shouldn't rush things. She'd been badly hurt in the past. *Take one day at a time, cariad*, as Nan would say. But how could she when his was the last face she imagined before dropping off to sleep each night and the first one she thought of when she opened her eyes each morning? This was going to be their first Christmas together and she hoped, no, she knew, it would be like this for every Christmas to come.

'A special day today. What do you think of the boats?' Yiannis said, nodding his head towards the quayside.

She turned around and looked across the harbour where twinkling lights adorned every vessel, from the modest fishing boats that brought in the much-needed hauls of fresh fish each morning to the luxury yachts owned by wealthy Athenians.

'It's magical, Yiannis. They really go to town on this, don't they?' said Alexandra.

'Go to town?' Her boyfriend raised one eyebrow as he always did when he didn't understand.

Alexandra smiled. 'It means they've taken a lot of trouble. Made a lot of effort.'

Yiannis had explained to her beforehand about the long-held tradition of decorating boats as part of the Greek Christmas activities, but she had not been prepared for how spectacular it was.

'It is because Péfka is an island and Greece is a maritime country. Decorating boats is particularly important for them. More important than decorating Christmas trees. That is quite new here on the island.'

To the left of the quayside, she noticed a large sailing ship where the full sails were festooned with tiny lights, sparkling like diamonds against the indigo sky. The hull of the ship was also lit up and its tall mast looked like an illuminated cross.

'Ah, you have spotted the Péfka galleon. That is unique to this island. It is normally found in a boatyard over on the mainland as a museum piece, but every year it is decorated and sails across from Porto Nikos to Péfka. At six o'clock in the evening on December 6th, the lights are lit for the first time.'

'Why December 6th?' Alexandra asked.

'Today is the feast of Saint Nikolaos, the patron saint of sailors and fishermen. It is said he worked hard to save sailors from the angry seas. The galleon coming to Péfka is to bring luck to all the island's sailors. Porto Nikos is named after him, of course.'

'What a lovely story,' said Alexandra. 'I do enjoy hearing about all your traditions.' She leaned across the table and kissed him.

Yiannis took her hand. 'Well, this is your home now. You are half Greek, and you should know about your homeland.'

A small knot formed in her stomach. Was this her real home now, not Wales? She knew Yiannis was right, but the guilt at not going home to see her grandmother and sister was still a niggle she'd have to deal with.

'Here comes our food,' he said.

They both tucked in and Alexandra hadn't realised how hungry she was. Working in the studio, she hadn't noticed the time until it had been too late for a proper lunch and she'd ended up just having a baklava dripping in honey and a coffee.

'This is delicious, Yiannis.' Alexandra had chosen her favourite moussaka again. 'To think I hadn't ever tasted aubergines when I arrived and now, I can't get enough of them.'

Yiannis laughed. 'We do have other meat other than lamb, you know?'

'I wonder what Papa is planning for Christmas dinner.'

'You'll have to wait and see.' Yiannis winked at her. 'But it's definitely not turkey.'

The next week passed quickly and Alexandra worked tirelessly to fulfil her Christmas orders. As she was taking a tray of her hand-thrown blue-green bowls through to the outside kiln room, a strong gust of wind blew up with such a force it smashed the door shut.

‘Nooo!’ she screamed, trying to keep the tray level.

The large *mati* hanging on the outside of the door fell onto the stone-paved area and shattered into shards of royal blue glass. One of the bowls also fell off and broke as it hit the hard surface. She took the remaining bowls to the storeroom and returned to clear up the mess.

The *mati* was the first thing she’d bought when she’d moved in to her studio. Everywhere on the island, she’d seen blue glass ornaments of concentric circles hanging in doorways. It was said that the evil eye in Greece was a ‘look’ or ‘stare’ believed to bring bad luck for the person it was directed at for reasons of envy or dislike. Yiannis had told her the *mati* was a talisman that was meant to protect you from these evil spirits. She tried to reassure herself. *I’m sure it will be just like the breaking of a mirror bringing you bad luck for seven years at home. Just an old wives’ tale.* But it didn’t stop her wondering what was to come.

A few days later, once she’d made a replacement bowl and closed her order book, Alexandra began work on her father’s Christmas present. Her idea was to make ceramic crib figures as a personal gift. She wanted the present to be unique, and she modelled the simple stylised figures in fine porcelain clay, making sure the proportions were right and allowing them to dry out extremely slowly until they were ready for firing. She'd worked in porcelain before and knew the figures would be special. With the sheen of the white glaze she'd chosen, they would be delicate, silky to the touch and made with love for her father. She stacked the kiln with care after checking for any drying out cracks and, as she sealed the door and turned up the temperature on the kiln, she closed her eyes and made a wish as she always did.

Two days later, she opened the kiln door and promptly burst into tears. One of the kings and Joseph had exploded, and it looked as if two shepherds had toppled over and lost an arm and a head, too. It was a disaster.

'*Kaliméra*!' It was Yiannis, calling from the kitchen. He had his own key now he was spending so much time here. Alcxandra came out of the studio holding the broken figures and began sobbing again.

'Whatever is it, *agápi mou*?' Yiannis took Alexandra in his arms and kissed the top of her head.

'Look,' she said through hot tears. 'Papa's gift. It's ruined.'

Yiannis took the broken pieces from her. 'You have time to remake these. The other figures are good, eh?'

Alexandra nodded. 'I should have started earlier. I wanted to get all my orders up to date so I could concentrate on Papa's present. I was sure I hadn't trapped any air in them. I don't think I have enough porcelain left. That blasted *mati*!'

Yiannis looked puzzled. 'What about it?'

'The *mati* over the back door smashed. First, I had to remake a commission piece I broke and now this. The old saying about bringing bad luck can't be true, surely? They say bad things come in threes, too. What else is going to go wrong?'

Yiannis fumbled in his pocket and brought out a bunch of keys. He took them off the key ring from which hung an enamel *mati*. 'Here. You will have no more bad luck. You must have this until you buy another one for your door,' he said.

Alexandra's features softened again. He placed the *mati* on the key holder next to the back door.

'Let me help you. I'm almost done with my orders and at least olive wood doesn't explode, does it?'

Alexandra smiled. Yiannis owned the woodturners in the village and his olive wood creations were famous not only on Péfka but in shops in Porto Nikos and surrounding towns, too.

'That's better. Nothing is as bad as you think. You said you got the special clay from the pottery in Ermione? Let me go and buy another bag for you, eh?'

Alexandra dried her eyes and then looked up at Yiannis and kissed him. *What would she do without this lovely man?* They moved into the sitting room and found the sofa where they resumed their kissing. She broke away and rubbed his cheek.

'You've got clay dust all over your face from me.'

'Why don't you shut up the studio and give yourself a break from working? That is what I came to tell you. Get your coat and some walking shoes,' suggested Yiannis.

The air was decidedly colder as Yiannis drove the scooter further in-land. In the distance, Alexandra saw a dense dark green patch on the side of the hill that contrasted with the rest of the landscape. Yiannis brought the scooter to a halt on the narrow road.

'See there,' he said, pointing. 'That is why Péfka got its name, the island of pines. Come on.'

He started up the scooter again and as they gathered speed, Alexandra's long, dark flowed out behind her. The patch of dark green turned out to be a densely planted area of pines, ranging from rows of saplings up to more mature trees.

'You said you wanted a real tree to decorate. You said how much you hated the artificial trees you've seen on Péfka,' said Yiannis. 'These are grown to make the retsina you love so much.'

'I do now!' Alexandra remembered how it taken her a long while to enjoy the unique taste of the wine. She watched as Yiannis went to the pannier on the back of the scooter and took out a large plastic bag and a trowel.

'We can't just dig one up,' said Alexandra. 'This must belong to someone. They didn't grow naturally in these rows.'

Yiannis asked her to choose. They were nothing like the Christmas fir trees they had back in Wales but, even though the shape was completely wrong, at least they were living. She chose one about the same height as her and knew exactly which of her garden pots it would fit in.

'I know the owner. He said I can steal a small one for you.'

Alexandra's mouth dropped open. 'If he knows, then it's not stealing!'

Yiannis dug carefully around the base of the tree and loosened the rich soil until the roots were visible. 'Open the bag for me, please. We must get it back to the studio and you can plant it tonight. I brought a bag of soil from my place and left it by the store room.'

He'd thought of everything.

'This tree will thrive, you know. Because we steal it. Greeks believe plants and flowers, even trees, will only root if they are stolen.'

Alexandra laughed. She'd have to nurture this pine tree now after all the trouble Yiannis had gone to. 'You and your superstitions. I do love you, Yiannis.'

The decorated pine tree took pride of place in the corner of the room. The lustre of Alexandra's intricately carved snowflakes reflected the white fairy lights shining out from the dark green branches among the beautiful olive wood ornaments Yiannis had made for her. She smiled as she remembered the gaudy tinsel, shiny baubles and homemade trinkets of Nan's Christmas trees. It had always been a family tradition that the weekend before Christmas, she and Claire could decorate the tree without any help from the adults once the coloured lights were in place. She picked up the Christmas card that had arrived from her nan that morning. The vintage Christmas tree image on the front was how she imagined Nan's would be again this year. She forced down a lump in her throat. On Christmas morning this year, Vasillis would be picking up her and Yiannis from the quayside in Porto Nikos and they would all be spending Christmas Day with her father and staying the night.

It was Christmas Eve and both she and Yiannis had closed their shops and studios.

After delivering the last of her bowls to customers, she spent the afternoon wrapping presents. The crib figures were individually packed in layers and layers of paper, and the box placed in the centre of her case surrounded by clothes to ensure it was safe. Everything was done and she got ready to meet Yiannis at his apartment.

Light was failing fast as Alexandra walked down the hill from her studio. The sky had turned a deep apricot as the sun's orb sank further into the horizon and the lights in the harbour gave the place a magical feel. A group of young boys had congregated at the door of the woodturners and, as she approached,

Yiannis opened the door to them. He said something to the children in Greek and Alexandra understood that he'd asked them to step aside to let her in. One child, who looked about ten, carried a model boat lit up with a tiny blue light from a miniature lamp inside. It had been painted gold and he shook it to show it was full of coins. Yiannis laughed and pretended to hide what was in the wooden bowl he was holding. The other children had triangles and small drums.

'You've arrived at the right time, *agápi mou*,' said Yiannis. 'You will hear the *Kálanda*. Today, it is the carols for Christmas. If the boys sing well, we give them nuts or dried figs or, if they are exceptionally good, drachmae.'

Alexandra stood by her boyfriend's side while the young children sang and played their instruments. When the carol singing finished, Alexandra clapped and Yiannis held out the bowl that was full of sweets, nuts and dried fruit. The boys took turns to put their hands in, and the older boy who held the boat delved in deep and drew out a drachma coin. Yiannis laughed and offered the others to do the same. The boys turned to go, all saying *efharistó* before moving on to the next cottage along the street.

Yiannis took Alexandra's hand and led her upstairs to the apartment over his workshop. It had belonged to his father before him, but Yiannis had taken over the wood turning business when Vasillis had retired and moved to the mainland. The room was softly lit and through the window overlooking the square there was an orange glow from the street lamps. They sat down together on the large leather sofa and Alexandra noticed the low table was laid with two glasses and an already opened bottle of retsina. Yiannis poured and handed her a glass.

'This is the start of your first Greek Christmas. Let's drink to a happy time with your Greek family. *Ya mas*!'

They clinked their glasses and Alexandra's eyes sparkled.

'I'm so excited. I can't wait for tomorrow to come,' she said.

They began kissing and familiar feelings stirred within her. Yiannis planted feathery kisses on her neck and earlobe. She tingled with pleasure.

Yiannis sat up and took Alexandra's face in both hands. 'I love you, Alexandra, and I want to spend the rest of my life with you.'

‘I feel the same. You mean everything to me. I can’t imagine life without you,’ she said, pulling him in towards her. Yiannis broke free and took a small leather box from his pocket, opening it to reveal a beautiful ring.

‘Then, please will you marry me, *agápi mou*? I think in Wales I should kneel on one knee. Is that right?’

Alexandra gasped. Her eyes misted with tears, her pulse racing. There was silence.

Yiannis got up and sat close to her. ‘You are not happy? I’ve made a mistake?’

‘No, you haven’t. And yes, yes, *YES*! I’ll marry you. Oh, Yiannis.’ Tears trickled down Alexandra’s cheeks as Yiannis placed the gold ring on the third finger of her left hand. She took in the detail of the gold band with shoulders intricately carved with the pattern of the Greek key on which stood a faceted aquamarine in the palest turquoise. She hugged him again. ‘It’s beautiful. I absolutely love it. How did you know it would fit?’

‘It belonged to Mamá. I borrowed your silver Greek ring to know the size and got a jeweller in Ermione to alter it. I hope you don’t mind it is not new. You are sure, eh? It meant so much to her, and she and Papa had an incredibly happy marriage. I want that for us, too.'

Alexandra couldn't stop admiring her ring. Knowing how much it meant to Yiannis made it even more special. 'Kyria Guikas. Doesn't it sound wonderful?'

'Getting down on one knee is the Welsh way, but here in Greece we have to ask the girl's father. It is what I have done. I went to see Stelios a few weeks ago and he is very happy his daughter is marrying a "good Greek boy" as he called me. Papa is delighted, too. It was he who suggested you had Mamá's ring. He says she would have loved you, Alexandra.'

Now it was his eyes that welled with tears. They both knew the pain of losing their mothers at a young age. Alexandra squeezed his hand and they sat for a few moments, deep in thought.

'Come on. We have wine to drink.' Yiannis refilled their glasses.

Soon afterwards, their kissing became more urgent and Yiannis led Alexandra into his bedroom where the lights were already dimmed and fragrant candles flickered on a bedside table. They fell onto the bed and undressed each other slowly before they made love with a passion Alexandra had never experienced before. Afterwards, they lay in each other's arms, just enjoying being with one another.

'Our first time as an engaged couple,' she said, planting a kiss on his lips.

'I suppose we'd better get dressed,' said Yiannis. 'I'll pack my things. I've booked the horse and carriage taxi to pick us up from your place in the morning in time for us to catch the ten o'clock ferry.'

Alexandra was too excited to sleep that night. She was already making wedding plans and wondering what her nan and Claire would say. She had no worries they would be happy for her. Hadn't her nan told her to follow her dreams? She looked across at the handsome man sleeping next to her and had no doubt he was part of her dreams. Light was creeping in through the blinds when she did fall into a deep sleep. She woke to find Yiannis shaking her.

'*Kalá Christoúgenna*, Alexandra.' He kissed her cheek. 'We've overslept. The taxi will be here in less than an hour.'

With that, the phone rang, and Alexandra got up to answer it whilst Yiannis rushed around.

'*Kaliméra*? Oh, Nan. You've beaten me to it. Happy Christmas to you, too.' Alexandra's throat tightened. 'I've got some news. Guess what? Yiannis proposed last night. Yes, of course I said yes. You're happy for me, aren't you?'

She listened to her nan telling her to have a lovely Greek Christmas.

'Yes, you too. I've got to go. I'll ring you in a day or so.'

The carriage, decorated with flowers and tiny lights arrived dead on 9.30 and they were soon at the quayside, waiting for the passenger ferry to take them across to Porto Nikos. Although it was cold, they sat up on deck and watched as the buildings on the mainland became more defined. The swell on the sea was strong and Alexandra began to feel queasy.

'I wish I'd woken up in time to eat some breakfast,' she said. 'It's all right for you, Yiannis Guikas. You got ready in lightning speed and managed a pastry and coffee.'

'This is what I have to get used to, is it? My fiancée taking hours to get herself ready. Here, just as well I brought this for you.' Yiannis handed Alexandra a sesame roll.

'Look, there's your papa!' The boat was nearing the jetty and Alexandra stood and walked to the rail, waving. 'Vasillis!'

A distinguished looking man who resembled an older version of Yiannis was leaning on the bonnet of an old silver-coloured car. He waved back and walked towards the gangway, arriving just as the ferry arrived at the quayside.

'*Kaliméra*! Congratulations, Alexandra.' Vasillis kissed his future daughter-in-law on both cheeks and shook his son's hand. 'She said "yes" then.'

He took their bags and placed them in the boot of the car. Alexandra sat in the back and enjoyed hearing father and son catch up on their news. She could now understand most of what they were saying in Greek, and it was clear she was very welcome in the Guikas family.

'Papa has already planned how many babies we are going to have, whether they are going to be boys or girls and is thinking of good Greek names for them.'

'I think we need to slow down, Vasillis.' Alexandra laughed.

The sky was now very overcast and, as they got higher up into the mountains, they could see snow in the distance. Vasillis stopped at the vantage point where she'd first seen her father's house on the journey to meet him for the first time. Then, in bright sunlight, it had been colour of pale cinnamon, with the terracotta ridged tiles clearly visible in the clear air. Today the house merged more in the background with an eerie feel. Alexandra couldn't wait to arrive and get inside in the warm.

'Not long now, *agápi mou.*' Yiannis turned to her and smiled. 'It looks like snow, so you may get the white Christmas you'd like after making all those snowflakes after all.'

It wasn't long before Vasillis was driving up to the large iron gates that opened automatically in front of them. As the car followed the lemon scree drive, sun peeped from behind a steel-grey cloud and the house was bathed in a clear light. Stelios Simonides was waiting for them in the heavy oak doorway. Alexandra rushed out of the car into his outstretched arms.

'Happy Christmas, Papa.'

'*Kalá Christoúgenna, agápi mou.*' Her father greeted his friend Vasillis and Yiannis and led them inside. Yiannis helped his father unpack the boot of the car and they both carried in boxes of food.

'Come. And welcome. I've put you in the front room just above here, Alexandra, and you, Yiannis, are with your papa in the room overlooking the olive grove.'

Alexandra and Yiannis took the bags upstairs, and Vasillis followed Stelios into the kitchen.

'No chance to sleep together tonight with my fiancée, then,' whispered Yiannis when he'd returned.

Alexandra grinned. 'You'll just have to behave. Wait here whilst I get Papa's Christmas present.'

By the time they joined both fathers in the kitchen, plates of baklava and oblong-shaped *melomakarono* covered in chopped walnuts were laid out on the work units, along with the customary *Christopsomo*, the special Christmas bread Yiannis had told Alexandra about. The smell of cinnamon, oranges and cloves hung in the warm air next to the huge oven where the Christmas dinner was cooking. She looked around at the other surfaces and gasped.

'A Christmas cake! I don't believe it. It even has a snow scene like Claire and I used to do at Nan's. And mince pies.' She picked up a royal blue glass bottle. 'You've even managed to get hold of Harvey's Bristol Cream.' Alexandra hugged her father. 'Here, this is for you, Papa,' she said, handing him the carefully wrapped box of crib figures.

'Go on through to the sitting room. We can open presents in there.'

Stelios opened the double doors and Alexandra gasped, unable to believe her eyes. Waiting in the room was Alexandra's nan, Sadie, and her sister, Claire.

'Nan!' squealed Alexandra. 'I don't believe it. Claire! Why didn't you both tell me?'

Tears streamed down their faces and, for a moment, the three of them stood in the middle of the room, hugging each other.

'We were sworn to secrecy by your papa,' said her nan. 'He wanted it to be a joint Greek and Welsh Christmas for you.'

Alexandra looked over at her father and saw that he, too, had tears in his eyes.

'So, this morning when you phoned …'

'She was ringing from here,' said Claire. 'Come on, show us your ring. I've got to be bridesmaid, mind.'

Alexandra held out her left hand and the aquamarine ring sparkled as the sunlight shone through the floor-to-ceiling windows.

'It's beautiful, *cariad*, really beautiful. So special as it belonged to Yiannis's mama and it was your mam's favourite colour. Congratulations. Claire, go and get our little gift for them, will you?'

Claire took a long, narrow shaped gift from the sideboard and handed it to Alexandra.

She read the label aloud. 'To Alexandra and Yiannis, Congratulations on your engagement. With all our love, Nan and Claire. You open it, Yiannis.' Alexandra handed it to him. 'But wait!' She turned to her sister and nan. 'You didn't know until we spoke this morning. I don't understand!'

Everyone else in the room laughed.

'But they did, *agápi mou*. You don't think I would have proposed without asking the most important person in your life? In Greece, we must have the father's agreement, but I knew I had to ask Sadie as well,' explained Yiannis. 'Luckily for me, she said she was happy.' Yiannis unwrapped the gift and held up a beautifully carved love spoon, with two hearts engraved with the initials *A* and *Y*.

'In Wales, these were given as love tokens.' Sadie pointed out each part on the design. 'The hearts are obviously for love, the bell here is for marriage, the knot symbolises everlasting love and see the little balls inside the frame? They signify how many children, you'll have.'

'Did you say we'd have three, Papa?' Yiannis laughed, and Alexandra thought briefly of the broken *mati. Maybe good things happened in threes, too?*

Yiannis handed the love spoon to Alexandra and stepped forward to hug first Sadie and then Claire. 'With three woodturners in the room, you could not have chosen a better gift. We will all see the craftsmanship and care that has gone into this.'

'I think we should pour some of Sadie's sherry and open the presents. This is the Welsh custom. In Greece, we normally open them on the feast of St Nikolaos on December 6th, but we were not all here then,' Stelios suggested.

Vasillis had already gone to the kitchen and brought in a tray with six glasses of sherry.

'But I haven't got any presents for Nan and Claire,' said Alexandra.

'No, but I have,' cut in Yiannis. 'They are from the both of us.' Yiannis handed out the presents but left it to Alexandra to hand her gift to her father. One by one, he unwrapped each figure.

'These are beautiful, *agápi mou*. I shall treasure them. Come here.'

Father and daughter stood for a moment, their arms around each other, but then Stelios looked towards the kitchen. 'I'd better check on the food,' he said. 'Sadie and I are doing a joint effort. We're having pork, Greek style – no turkey, I'm afraid – and lots of vegetables. Then Sadie tells me you always have a special pudding, Christmas pudding, and brandy sauce. I have no idea what that is, but I have provided the brandy. Metaxa, of course!'

It was getting dark as they were about to file into the dining room, and Vasillis called them to look out of the window. 'Look, it's snowing! You got your white Christmas after all, Alexandra.'

Large soft flakes settled on the ground, forming a white carpet that sparkled in the lights from the house. Alexandra's first Christmas in Greece was truly magical. Surrounded by all the people she loved, it was turning into the best Christmas ever.

** The End **

Find out more about Jan Baynham and her novels here: https://www.rubyfiction.com/productcat/jan-baynham/

Jan's novels include: *Her Mother's Secret* & *Her Sister's Secret.*

Substitute Santa
Carol Thomas

'It can't be!' Beth's eyes went wide as she looked at the teacher who had led her son's class into the school hall. Tom Eden. It couldn't be, and yet the rush of her pulse and the sight before her told her that it most definitely was. She hadn't seen him for nine years and, after what had happened on that final day in Switzerland, she hoped she'd never see him again. Spotting the scar on his cheek, she swallowed.

Beth tried to focus on the class as they followed him in, ready to take their places. Dressed in an array of brightly coloured costumes, they emanated nervous excitement, as their eyes searched the audience for their parents and grandparents. Beth's son, Ollie, smiled and waved. His cheeky face was the perfect distraction, until he failed to stop in his place and walked straight into Tom. *Oh no!* It was all too much; her past colliding with the here and now in a packed school hall that felt claustrophobic even before Tom Eden put in an appearance.

Beth looked at the exits and then back to Ollie. Could she think of a reason to leave and take him with her? No. Drawing attention to herself would be a mistake. She just needed to stay calm. The past was in the past; Tom had no reason to suspect Ollie was hers. As a substitute teacher, hopefully he would just be in Dapplebury Primary for the day, after which the affable Mrs Stone would be back and everything would return to normal.

Beth took a steadying breath. She knew she just had to sit back and see it through; Ollie had practised so hard and the performance would be an hour and a half, tops. This was his moment and that was all that was important. *You can do this*. But even as she thought the words, events of that crisp, bluebird morning on a snowy Swiss mountain began to play through her mind. Folding her arms, she adjusted her position in her seat. The narrator stood and welcomed everyone, before introducing the play. *Whoops-A-Daisy-Angel* was underway. Beth welcomed the distraction and determined to avoid looking directly at Tom. If she didn't make eye contact and draw attention to herself, he'd never know she was there.

An hour later, and she had to concede nothing said Christmas had arrived like watching a school nativity play. After all the years of making costumes, including an angel with a wonky halo and a camel whose hump wouldn't have looked out of place in

Notre Dame, the knowledge that this was Ollie's last nativity caused an ache in her chest and a lump to form in her throat.

She knew next year would be different. In key stage two, the Christmas performance was a billed as a carol service; though rumour had it, this meant an afternoon of listening to the children sing along to Christmas pop songs with a slightly American accent that had more to do with YouTube than their upbringing in the quaint English village of Dapplebury.

When at last the children burst into an enthusiastic but tuneless rendition of 'We Wish You a Merry Christmas', tears welled in her eyes and threatened to spill as Ollie pointed at her on the 'you' with a broad grin. Her heart swelled at the precious site. Seeing the other parents in the hall, watching their children and sharing the moment, she felt another ache in her chest. As the words 'and a happy new year' rang out with gusto, Beth clapped, along with every other adult in the hall. The children had done them proud, just as they did every year.

Stepping into the limelight without hesitation, Mr Eden stood to thank the children for their wonderful acting and reassured the parents that Mrs Stone hoped to make it back into school for the class Christmas party the next day. Beth did her best not to look in his direction and welcomed his words.

After a brief speech from the headteacher reminding them all to attend the Christmas fair between three-thirty and six, there was just time for a congratulatory hug for Ollie and a photograph – strictly of her own child and not to be shared on social media – before Beth was able to prepare herself to leave the hall. About to go, she felt a hand on her arm; she knew it was his even before she turned to meet Tom Eden's bright blue eyes. *Don't mention Switzerland; don't look at the scar.*

'Beth, it's you. I can't believe it. It's been …'

'Nine years,' she finished wishing she hadn't made it sound as if she'd been counting.

'It's so good to—'

'Yes, you too. But I'm really sorry. I've got to go.' Beth offered a small smile and gestured to the door.

'Of course. Me too.' Tom looked towards the class standing with the teaching assistant, waiting for him. 'But it really is good to see you.'

Beth felt as well as saw the affection in his smile and wondered how he still had a hold over her after all these years, and all she'd been through.

Leaving the warmth of the school hall, the chill in the air reminded her that snow was forecast. She shook her head; as if she needed any more of a reminder of the final day she and Tom had spent together in Switzerland. Attempting to push the memory aside, she slipped her gloves on and pulled her scarf up over her nose before heading into the village centre.

Christmas was always a busy time; her sister had kindly offered to open the cafe for her, but she didn't want to leave her alone too long in case there was a mid-morning rush. Being a single parent wasn't easy, especially when it came to needing to be in two places at once.

A choir from the local college were dressed in Victorian costumes, singing 'O Come All Ye Faithful' in the square, raising money for the hospice. Despite the fact she knew she couldn't afford it, Beth put a generous donation in the bucket. Pulling her coat a little tighter around herself, she headed across the cobbled street to Serendipity, the café she'd opened the year after losing her husband. The windows were misted with condensation causing the lights from the Christmas tree to spread into patterns etching across the glass.

The rich aroma of coffee welcomed her as she opened the door. The warmth and the smell of mince pies cooking enveloped her as much as her sister's hug.

'Thanks so much for opening up for me.' Glancing round the café, Beth smiled at her regulars.

'You're welcome. How was the play?' Mae had brought Beth a mug of coffee and barely gave her chance to remove her scarf and gloves before she spoke.

'Wonderful. Ollie remembered all his lines; there was just one minor hiccup when he insisted on taking the gold back with him to his place instead of giving it to the baby Jesus, other than that it was all good. Except …' Beth hesitated for a moment, but then shook her head and hung her coat on the coat stand. Behind the counter, she washed her hands and picked up an apron.

Mae looked at her, waiting. 'You're really building the suspense here.'

'It doesn't matter.' Beth took her coffee with thanks and sipped it, realising how much she'd needed the hit of caffeine.

Mae moved to the other side of the counter and sat on a stool. 'You can't just put that out there and then change the subject. Except ...' Mae emulated Beth's wistful expression and tone as she spoke. 'Except what?'

Beth let out a sigh. Why had she mentioned anything in front of her sister? Now she'd have to talk about Tom, and Mae could always read her too well. She bit her lip hesitantly, before speaking. 'Ollie's substitute teacher.'

'Oh! A substitute teacher on play day. Was it carnage?'

'No, like I said, it was great. He had everything under control.' Of course he did, he always did! And she had liked that about him.

'So, what was the problem?'

'It was Tom … Tom Eden.' Beth felt her cheeks colour as she said his name and watched as realisation dawned in Mae's eyes.

'Switzerland Tom?'

Beth covered her face with her hands and nodded.

Mae leaned across the counter. 'Did he mention—'

'The fact I am the worst seasonaire—'

'Chalet girl!'

'Seasonaire, ever. No.' Beth moved her hands and spotted a table of customers preparing to leave. Welcoming the opportunity to escape Mae's gaze, she went to collect their crockery and wipe down the table. When she returned to the counter, it was clear Mae wasn't ready to let the subject go.

'I think you're being too hard on yourself. There must have been others who had a massive crush on the son of their boss. I'm pretty sure I've even seen a film where a chalet girl does just that.'

'Yes, but the girl in that film doesn't attempt to show off to the son of her boss by insisting he join her on an early morning skiing trip, lose control of her skis, flail towards him like a wild woman, not only knocking him over but also slicing across his cheek with the edge of her ski. Believe me, when you mix crisp white snow and blood, the scene goes from picture postcard perfect to pandemonium and looking like a massacre in no time!'

'Wasn't he—'

'Assisted down the mountain by the ski patrol? Yes! Right before I got sacked and returned to England.'

'And you haven't spoken to him since?'

'Oh, I have now. He just said hello to me.' Beth drank down her coffee, thinking how surreal it was to have seen Tom in the village primary. But then she had known he hadn't wanted to join his father's company. He had confessed he wanted to be a teacher during one of their late-night conversations.

'He remembered you?'

'Of course he remembered me. He's got a scar across his cheek and probably had to have therapy before ever going near a ski slope again.'

Mae was smiling with a suspicious glint in her eyes. 'Did he seem like he was harbouring resentment or was he pleased to see you? Oh, and how does the scar look?'

Beth let out a long breath. 'Honestly, he smiled and seemed genuinely pleased to see me. And his scar was faint and … sort of sexy.'

'Oh my goodness, this is perfect. You still like him, don't you?'

Beth had seen that matchmaking look in her sister's eyes before; she was incorrigible.

'Mae, don't. You know I'm not interested.'

'Tom Eden is here, in Dapplebury, and you're not interested? I don't believe you.'

'Seriously? I'm a widow. What would it say if I still had a thing for Tom Eden, the person I liked before I met Jack, before we had our beautiful boy, before we married and before I lost him? We went through so much together. I can't just rewind the past nine years.'

‘It would say you’re human and, while you truly loved your husband and he loved you, you know he would want you to keep living.’ Mae reached over and held Beth’s hand. ‘It’s been two years. Hell, my husband’s alive, but if Gary Barlow walked through that door, believe me, I’d be tempted.’

‘Why would Gary Barlow be in my café?’

Mae rolled her eyes. ‘You know what I mean. Sometimes someone comes along who makes your nerve endings come alive. Gary Barlow does it for me ... or Howard ... or Mark … I’m not sure about Robbie these days but—’

Beth coughed.

‘But that’s besides the point. You missed your moment with Tom Eden, maybe this is a second chance. Before the … incident, you felt there was a connection between the two of you, didn’t you?’

Beth thought about the conversations they’d shared and the secret smiles when in the company of his family; the moments their eyes had met, and the heat and intensity of the briefest touch of their skin as they’d brushed past each other. Tom had felt it too, she was sure he had. ‘Yes.’

‘You, more than anyone, knows that life is too bloody short. It’s okay to be happy, Beth. You deserve to be happy.’ Mae smiled.

Beth wiped her eyes and took a breath before squeezing her sister’s hand.

‘He could be with someone else. Have you thought about that?’

‘He could be single. I bet you’ve thought about that.’

‘He’s only here on supply. It could be another nine years before I even see him again.’

‘More reason to seize your moment. Aren’t you collecting Ollie?’

‘No, he’s going to his friend Jake's for tea. I’m meeting them later at the Christmas fair.’

‘Then you’ll see Tom there.’

‘Why would a substitute teacher hang around for the Christmas fair?’

‘Because I think this is meant to be,’ Mae spoke with the confidence of a side-street fortune teller, causing Beth to shake her head.

As the door to the café opened, three of the Victorian carollers walked in brushing a light dusting of snow from their hair and shoulders. Beth greeted them with a smile and picked up two menus. Looking at Mae she whispered, 'Fine, if he's at the fair and something happens that suggests it's meant to be, I'll consider seizing my moment. But that's it. I'll *consider* it – that's all I'm promising.'

'That's all I'm asking!' Mae took the menus from Beth's hands and walked over to the customers, a wide grin on her face that Beth was sure was completely misplaced, especially as neither of those things were likely to happen.

By the time Beth reached the school, the hedgerow and the roof of the Victorian building were covered in a thick layer of snow. The path had been cleared and gritted but the snow continued to fall, attempting to settle. Beth dodged a few icy missiles hurled by children having a snowball fight just outside the school gates. Their squeals of excitement and laughter echoed through the crisp evening air.

Even as she entered the school grounds, Beth could see the Christmas fair was busy. It seemed every pupil and their family had waited until the last hour to turn up – it was, after all, the time the school musicians were set to play on stage, when the tombola would be half price and the raffle tickets would be drawn.

Seeing the bike shed had been made into a makeshift stable, Beth smiled. Below a sign that said, 'Parking reserved for Santa!' was a Shetland pony wearing a fleece-lined red blanket and a pair of antlers, munching through a trough of 'reindeer' food. She knew Ollie would love that and wondered if he'd already seen it. He still believed in the magic of Christmas; wondering if Tom might be inside, she questioned whether she did too. *Don't be ridiculous, you know he won't be here*. She shook her head; why had she let her sister put fanciful ideas in her mind?

Entering the hall, Beth could see signs to Santa's grotto and a variety of stalls offering children the opportunity to spend money winning back an array of items previously purchased and donated by their parents.

Spotting Jake's mum, Charlotte, in the crowd, Beth waved. The boys were having a go at the snowball shy.

'They're throwing snowballs for real outside the school.' Beth smiled as she approached them.

When Ollie turned, she could see chocolate on his face, a half empty jar of jazzies sweets in his hand and an assortment of small plastic toys hanging from his overflowing pockets.

‘Wow! You look like you’re having fun.’

‘Sorry. I did suggest saving the sweets for later.’ Charlotte grimaced.

‘Don’t worry at all. He looks like he’s had a brilliant time. I’ll have to return the favour and have Jake over next week.’

The boys cheered before Ollie told Beth everything they’d done so far, just as she thought he was going to pause for air, excitement filled his eyes, and he continued: ‘... and we’ve got to see Santa. We tried earlier but it was super busy.’

Beth glanced over to the queue for Santa’s grotto. The headteacher, Mrs Kemp, was dressed as an elf, keeping the children’s spirits up as they waited.

‘There’s only two families waiting now. Do you want to join the queue and I’ll fetch me and Charlotte some mulled wine? How does that sound?’

The boys didn’t hesitate and rushed over to the queue while Charlotte smiled. ‘Perfect! And it means they’ll be in one place for a while.’

Beth laughed and went to fetch two plastic cups of mulled wine. While it was non-alcoholic, the warm, sweet scents of cinnamon, cloves and citrus hit the spot as she took a sip and wound her way back through the busy hall to Charlotte.

'Where are the boys?'

'In seeing Santa. Ollie insisted they were big enough to go in alone!'

'Really?' Beth felt bereft at missing Ollie's face when he saw Santa. It always amazed her that pure belief meant the school library, bedecked in an array of sheets, net curtains, tinsel, glitter and fairy lights, made Ollie not recognise Mr Green the caretaker, who, admittedly, played a convincing Santa.

When the boys came out, they were smiling and already unwrapping their gifts. They were both delighted with the books they'd received.

'Did Santa ask what you wanted for Christmas?' Beth realised, having not gone into the grotto herself, she had missed out on the magical moment *and* being privy to Ollie's wish list that normally helped her ensure he wasn't disappointed when it came to unwrapping his stocking.

'Yes.'

'And what did you say?'

'I can't say.' Ollie pressed his lips together and folded his arms, tucking his book under his elbow.

'Santa won't mind you telling me.'

'No, it's a surprise, but it's okay, Mummy, Santa said he'd be happy to make my wish come true. Can we go and do the reindeer racers now?' Ollie was still talking as he headed off towards the stall, closely followed by Jake. The two boys weaved their way through the audience that had gathered to watch the musicians who were on stage performing 'Little Donkey'.

'No pressure then.' Beth looked at Charlotte and shrugged her shoulders.

'Ask Mrs Kemp. She took them in. I'm sure there's no elf confidentiality contract.' Charlotte laughed.

'That's a great idea. Do you mind watching Ollie just a little longer?'

Beth drank down her mulled wine and went to find the headteacher while Charlotte kept an eye on the boys. Being told Mrs Kemp and Santa were readying themselves to wave goodbye to the children from the bike-shed-stable after the raffle was called, Beth headed outside. Missing the heat from inside as she stepped out into the snow, she pulled her coat around herself.

Seeing Santa stroking the reindeer she went over and whispered, 'Mr Green. I hope you don't mind me asking, but what did Ollie ask for? Only you said you'd do your best to make his wish come true, and, well, he's had a lot to cope with over the last few years … making sure he has a happy Christmas is quite important to me.'

As the man in the Santa Claus suit turned to face her, Beth let out a gasp. 'Tom!'

His blue eyes glinted in the evening light. The fur of his red suit had a dusting of snow, and she quickly attempted to wipe away the flakes from her hair.

Checking there were no children in the vicinity before meeting her gaze Tom smiled, causing his white beard to lift a little, covering the tip of the scar Beth could see on his cheek. 'It's good to see you again.'

'But you're still here, and you're Santa.' Beth's mind needed to catch up with the sight before her.

'Yes, I'm the new deputy head, starting officially in January—'

'Oh!' So definitely not on supply then. He was in Dapplebury to stay.

'Yes, I was due to visit today, but with Mrs Stone being taken ill first thing, stepping in seemed the right thing to do. Of course, I didn't know then I'd be taking on this role too.' Tom patted his large belly.

Beth laughed and the "reindeer" nodded his head, causing the bells on his red velvet antlers to ring.

‘You’ve filled Mr Green’s boots well. He’s not ill too, is he?’

‘No, he’s fine and happy to take the year off. He was last seen brewing up another batch of mulled wine.’

‘Ah, it’s very good. I’ve just—’ Glancing in the direction of the hall, Beth remembered why she’d sought Santa out. She shook her head, trying to focus. It was strange. If she hadn't known the mulled wine was non-alcoholic, she could have sworn she felt a little drunk; her head felt light, while her pulse seemed to be beating a little too fast. Despite the falling snow, heat spread in her cheeks. ‘Anyway, I, umm … I wondered if you’d mind telling me what Ollie wished for? Only, you told him you’d be happy to make his wish come true, and that rather puts the pressure on me. So, what was it?’

Tom glanced around again, and Beth appreciated the fact he didn’t want to be caught out of character.

‘Don’t worry, I made a promise and I meant it. I really will do my best to make Ollie’s wish come true.’

Beth appreciated the gesture, but Tom was new to the village. He had no idea what she and Ollie had been through – how difficult it had been losing Jack.

‘Thank you, I appreciate it, I do. But Ollie’s happiness—’ *Oh no*! Tears were welling in her eyes, she was going to cry, in front of Tom Eden for goodness sake.

Tom looked at her, the smile in his eyes turning to concern. As he took off his glove and wiped a tear from her cheek, he sighed. ‘Ollie said he wants you to be happy again. He knows you’re still sad about losing his daddy and wants you to have someone to love you the way other mummies do.’ Tom’s voice was a whisper, but Beth could hear the compassion in his tone.

She let out a sob and put a hand to her mouth. Her emotions spiralled between sadness that she hadn’t hidden her feelings from Ollie and wonderment that he was such a kind and thoughtful boy that he had used his Christmas wish on her.

Tom took her hand in his and the touch sent her mind back to those stolen moments in Switzerland. ‘I know I shouldn’t have made promises, but when Ollie said he wanted you to be happy, I knew it was a wish I’d like to help come true. If you’ll let me. So, what do you say, Beth? Will you give me a chance? We could go on a proper date, or just a drink if you’re not ready for that, but either way, strictly no skis involved!' He ventured a smile.

Beth couldn't help the giggle that escaped her. She looked at Tom and thought about the promise she had made to her sister. Tom Eden was at the school fair dressed as Santa, standing in a make-shift stable next to a "reindeer", asking her out on a date while snow fell all around them. It definitely seemed like a sign she should seize her moment. Besides, Mae would never let her live it down if she didn't.

But as she stood there, her eyes holding his gaze, she realised none of those reasons were why she was saying yes. It was because, without doubt, she knew she wanted to get to know the man standing in front of her, she wanted to go on a date with him and, unless she was very much mistaken – it had been quite a while, after all – she very much wanted to kiss him.

Pulling him closer towards her, she smiled. 'I'd like that very much.' With their lips almost touching, she giggled at the feel of his white, fluffy beard. He went to move apologetically, but she pulled him back to her, kissing him regardless. The touch of his lips on hers felt exciting, new and different, causing her mind to spin and forgotten sensations to ripple through her body.

‘Wow! Santa, that was fast!’

Beth and Tom jumped apart at the sound of Ollie’s voice. As they turned to face him, Beth couldn’t help but smile at his wide eyes and beaming expression. ‘Hmm now, how do you suggest we explain this, Santa?’ she whispered.

‘It’s okay, Mummy. I know Mr Eden isn’t the real Santa. He’s just helping him out because the real Santa’s busy getting everything ready at the North Pole. Charlotte told me.’

Beth looked at Charlotte, who had followed Ollie out of the hall, and mouthed ‘thank you’. Charlotte winked. As the rest of the families began to leave, raffle and other prizes in hand, Tom, directed by Mrs Kemp, took his place to wave them goodbye and to wish them a very merry Christmas.

When, at last it was time for Beth and Ollie to leave, they walked along the path to the school gate.

‘That was like that song, Mummy. I saw you kissing Santa Claus.’

‘You’re cheeky!’ Beth smiled as Ollie giggled.

Leaving the warmth and noise of the school behind, they walked into the village streets. The cool air felt refreshing against Beth’s cheeks, while Ollie’s gloved hand felt warm nestled in hers. As she looked at the snow, glistening in the light from the streetlamps, everything felt fresh and new. She realised she felt happy; not because she'd shared a very lovely kiss with Tom Eden, or because she had agreed to go on a date with him, but because she was thinking of all she had to be thankful for. Her business was doing well, she had a wonderful – if not opinionated – sister onside, and Ollie, despite everything they had been through, was loving, kind-hearted and generous. For the first time in a long time, she was happy in the here and now, and looking forward, with excitement, to the future yet to come.

** The End **

Find out more about Carol Thomas and her novels here: https://www.rubyfiction.com/productcat/carol-thomas/

Carol's novels include: Maybe Baby & The Purrfect Pet Sitter.

Fairy Wishes and Christmas Kisses
Sharon Ibbotson

'So, the Santa here is a bit of a silver fox.'

With a groan, Holly looked up from her green and red striped tights, which were currently in a tangle somewhere between her calf and knee.

'I wish they'd make these things easier to get on,' she mumbled, before doing a double take. Leaning against the wall, in a glittery dress so big and bright it would give Glinda the Good Witch of the North a run for her money, stood a fairy.

A Christmas fairy.

'Who are you?' Holly asked, before frowning. 'Wait, are you the temp they sent for? Isobel or something ...?'

The fairy shrugged. 'Isobel. Sure. Why not?'

'Oh.' Holly looked her up and down. From the sparkling slippers on her feet to the puffed sleeves on her gown, Isobel looked like the living incarnation of the Sugar Plum Fairy. 'Nice costume. Is that from here or did you bring your own?'

Isobel looked down, almost confused. 'What, this old thing? It came with the job.'

Holly nodded, before looking ruefully at her tights again. 'Better than these things,' she murmured.

'I think they're sweet. You look cute in them,' Isobel said easily. Her eyes sparkled almost as brightly as the wand she tapped lightly on her glittery skirt. 'So, tell me about Santa. Is he single?'

Holly groaned again as she finished rolling up her tights and stepped into the green and gold elf boots that had bells on their curved toe caps.

'And these,' she moaned, shaking her foot at Isobel and hearing the merry ringing that followed. 'I hear these bells in my sleep, I swear to you.'

Isobel grinned. 'You should do that more often. You know that every time a bell rings a fairy gets its wings, right?'

Holly smiled back. 'Why, are you waiting for yours?'

Isobel smirked. 'Something like that. So, tell me about Santa ... I hear he's quite the looker.' Isobel paused. 'Under the fake beard and belly, I mean.' She paused again. 'They *are* fake, right? Because if they aren't ...'

Holly sighed, pulling on her elf hat. It too had a bell on the end, and for a moment, she looked enviously at Isobel in all her pink – but mercilessly silent – glitter.

'I mean, I'm not saying a bit of a belly is a dealbreaker, but all the same—'

'Stop, stop,' Holly begged, holding up her hand. 'Yes, the belly and beard are fake. And, yes ... Santa is ... *somewhat* attractive. You know, if you're into smouldering, obvious good looks and all that.' Holly paused, trying to push away an image of searching grey eyes and kissable lips. She stood taller. 'But look, listen to me, Isobel. You do not want to get involved with Jack North. Especially on your first day on the job.'

'Jack North?' Isobel's mouth dropped open. 'Santa's real name is ... Jack North?'

'Yes.'

'Jack North,' Isobel mused. 'How apt. How charming.'

Holly buttoned up her fur-trim jacket. With a sigh, she turned to the mirror for a final inspection. 'Trust me, there is absolutely nothing *charming* about Jack North.'

Isobel stared at her for a moment. 'Why Holly, don't tell me you've ...?' she trailed off suggestively.

'What?' Holly asked.

Isobel smirked. 'Already visited the *North Pole*?'

Holly blushed. 'Isobel!'

'Oh, don't worry, I get it, he's gorgeous.' Isobel leaned forward. 'So, tell me, are you two still ...?'

But Holly held up her hand. 'Nope. Not interested.' Her eyes narrowed. 'Trust me, Isobel, the only bell Jack North is ringing this year is the one that comes with his Santa costume. Now, come on. I've got a hundred and thirteen children to photograph with Santa before teatime.'

The grotto was thriving that evening. Carols rang out across the department store, while tasteful decorations hung across the walls and ceilings in a grand imitation of Santa's workshop. In the corner stood a Christmas tree, laden with tinsel, presents wrapped neatly underneath. And next to that, sitting on a large chair, bedecked with red velvet and paper stars, was Santa.

No. Not Santa. *Jack North.*

Holly refused to let him distract her, though she felt his gaze upon her frequently as she readied her camera. They were busy, and she didn't have time to think about anything other than angles and lighting. Occasionally, she would glance in his direction and meet his eyes, and it was like a bolt of lightning shooting through her spine. But then she would spin on her jingling boots and look in the other direction.

She was there for the kids, after all. Not him.

Definitely not him.

Holly liked working at Klein's Department store. She liked the merry atmosphere and the excited children visiting Santa in their Christmas jumpers or tartan dresses. A photographer by trade, December was always a lull for her wedding photography business, and Klein's paid her well for doing something she loved: capturing smiles and perfect moments.

Yes, she liked working at Klein's.

It was just a shame that Jack North did too.

Frowning, Holly snapped a picture of Santa, Isobel the Christmas fairy and two children in matching plaid pyjamas clutching teddy bears. It was a cute picture, and she could just imagine the smiles on people's faces when they saw it on their Christmas card, but still, there was something off about the picture.

Something was missing.

'I think that's break time,' she said, still puzzled, as the children left the room. 'Half an hour for lunch until the next group,' she told Isobel. 'Don't get any food on your costume though, okay, Isobel? Management will make you pay for the dry-cleaning.'

'Dry cleaning?' Isobel asked blankly.

‘Yeah.’ Holly nodded. ‘I bet a costume that good will set you back a pretty penny in laundry costs. Now go on, get something to eat.’

Exhaling deeply, Holly made her way to Jack’s side. ‘Hello, Santa,’ she said coolly.

Jack’s eyes glinted up at her. ‘Why, if it isn’t Santa’s favourite elf.’ She grimaced, but he looked at her seriously from beneath his red fur hat. ‘I mean it, Holly. How are you?’

‘Fine.’

‘Good,’ he murmured softly. ‘I’ve been worried. I haven’t seen you around much this year.’

‘I’ve been busy,’ she said tightly.

He nodded. ‘I just ... well, I thought you might have been avoiding me after what happened last Christmas and—’

‘Avoiding you?’ Holly interjected. ‘You think I’ve been avoiding you?’ She shook her head in disgust. ‘Oh, that’s rich when you’re the one who kissed me and then never called.’

‘What?’ he asked sharply, sitting up. But Holly looked down, away from him and those damnably gorgeous grey eyes.

‘No,’ she said abruptly. ‘No, I’m going to be professional about this.’ She took a deep breath.

'Look, with the next lot of kids I need you to angle your head up to the light. I'm losing your face under the hat and beard.'

'No, wait, Holly—'

But Holly refused to listen. She turned her back on him, going back to her camera and the safety of life through a lens.

By mid-afternoon, Holly's temper was frayed. She'd snapped picture after picture of happy children with Santa and Isobel, and although they were good, there was still something off about them that she couldn't place. More than that, Santa seemed tense, watching Holly with piercing eyes.

'I need ten minutes,' she snapped at one point after another disappointing shoot, stalking in the direction of the changing room.

'Holly!' Jack called out after her, but Holly ignored him.

See how he liked it, she thought bitterly.

She stood in the changing room, unaccountably on the verge of tears, when she felt a hand on her shoulder.

'Hey,' a voice spoke gently, and Holly looked up into the soft eyes of Isobel. She was still in her fairy costume, and Holly chewed on her lip, wondering how anyone could be that *good* with make-up. Isobel's skin was luminescent, as though made of magic itself, while her eyes were flawlessly shimmering.

'Hey,' Holly said, straightening quickly and wiping at her eyes.

'You okay?' Isobel asked.

'Yes, of course.'

Isobel frowned. 'Look, I know we've only just met, but you don't *seem* okay. Not at all.'

Holly shook her head. 'I'm fine, honestly, I'm just ...' She paused, suddenly spellbound by the sheer concern evident in Isobel's eyes. 'I'm just a little in love with Santa, is all,' she finished miserably.

Isobel sighed. 'Yes, I thought as much.'

'Did you?'

Isobel shrugged. 'Well, you've been staring at him longingly all morning, and the tension between you is so thick I would need an industrial grade blade to cut it.'

Holly couldn't help her face from falling. 'I didn't know my feelings for Jack were so obvious.'

'Well, they are,' Isobel replied, before leaning closer to Holly. 'But then, so are his feelings for you.'

‘Wh ... what?’ Holly asked tremulously. ‘Jack isn’t ... I mean, he and I ... he didn’t even *call* me after what happened between us.’

‘No?’ Isobel asked, surprise in her eyes. ‘That’s strange. Did you ask him why?’

‘And embarrass myself further?’ Holly shuddered. ‘No. I didn’t ask him.’

‘Maybe you should,’ Isobel offered. ‘It would clear the air between you, if nothing else.’

‘There’s nothing to clear,’ Holly insisted, but Isobel gave her an understanding smile loaded with sympathy.

‘If that were true,’ Isobel said, ‘you wouldn’t be hiding away here nearly in tears, would you now?’

Holly took a deep, shuddering breath. ‘Maybe,’ she murmured softly. ‘Maybe I should.’

She stared at Isobel for a moment, considering her as though for the first time. ‘I never understood the association of fairies with Christmas,’ she said suddenly. ‘Like, I get why Santa is important, and his elves, and Mrs Claus and gingerbread men and all the rest ... but fairies? What do fairies have to do with Christmas?’

Isobel smiled. ‘Oh, we make wishes come true,’ she said flippantly.

Holly resisted the urge to roll her eyes. 'You are alarmingly good at your job. You're almost making me believe in nonsense like fairies and wishes coming true.'

Isobel stared at her. 'But wishes do come true,' she insisted. 'Did you make a Christmas wish this year, Holly?'

'No,' Holly admitted, 'I'm a grown up, Isobel. I don't believe in wishes or fairies.'

Isobel looked puzzled. 'How odd,' she said. 'But if you didn't make a wish then it must have been ...' she trailed off, and Holly looked at her quizzically.

'What are you talking about?'

'Nothing.' Isobel suddenly brightened, dusting an invisible stray piece of glitter from her dress. 'Well, shall we get back to it? You have a schedule to stick to, after all.' She gave Holly a beaming smile. 'And a Santa to talk to.'

When the last child for the day was photographed, Holly turned her camera off with a sigh. The prints were digital and instantly forwarded to the clients, so there was no need for her to spend hours at her laptop editing. She was looking forward to a night spent mindlessly in front of her television, a glass of wine in hand.

But first she had Santa to talk to.

With a deep breath she approached Jack, who was pulling off the outer layers of his Santa outfit.

'Jack,' she said softly, and his grey eyes immediately met hers.

'Holly,' he returned, before he cleared his throat. 'That was a hard shift today. Well done.'

'You too,' she said. 'I don't know if I was any good today, though. Every single picture I took ... there was something strange about them.'

'You did look like you were struggling at points,' Jack admitted, before he cleared his throat again. 'I wondered if ... that is, I was worried ... that maybe you were distracted by me?'

Holly instantly blushed. 'I, umm ...'

'The last time I saw you I was kissing you,' Jack said softly. 'And if I'd had my way, I'd still be kissing you now.'

'But you ... you never called me,' Holly stammered. 'You kissed me and then never got in touch. I just assumed you ...' she paused, 'that you hadn't enjoyed it. That you regretted it.'

'Holly, no, no, no,' Jack said quickly, stepping towards her. 'I *loved* kissing you. I'd wanted to kiss you for years. Since the first day you walked into this grotto in your elf shoes. That was it for me.'

Holly stared at him. 'Then why didn't you call me?'

'Because you didn't give me your number,' Jack said softly.

'You could have Googled my business and found my work number,' Holly told him, but he gave a tiny huff, shaking his head.

'Holly, when you kiss a woman and she doesn't give you her number, well, that's a pretty big sign that she isn't interested. And what was I going to do? Call your work number and look like a fool all over again?'

Holly's mouth fell open. It had never occurred to her to give Jack her number. She'd always assumed, having worked together so long, that he'd already had it. 'You can have my number now, if you like?' she offered, and Jack smiled.

'How about once I'm out of my costume and you're out of yours, we go and get a drink somewhere?' he asked her. 'You can give me your number there.'

Holly bit down a grin. 'I would like that,' she said. 'I would like that very much.'

Jack nodded, though Holly could see the smile playing on his lips. 'Although we've been so busy today we might both be asleep on our feet after a drink or two,' he remarked. 'If the temp had come in, that might've made things easier. Klein's have promised she'll be in tomorrow though.'

Holly froze. 'What do you mean? Isobel?'

Jack nodded as he pulled off his red velvet waistcoat. 'Yes, she called in sick earlier. But she'll be here tomorrow.'

Something a little like disbelief ran down Holly's spine. 'But she was ...' she began, before she stopped herself. 'Will you just wait here?' she asked Jack.

He nodded, watching curiously as Holly sprinted back to her camera and turned it on. She pulled up the last few photos of the day, her mouth falling open as she did so.

Isobel wasn't in any of them.

Quickly, she pulled up the pictures from the morning shoot. No Isobel. Stunned, Holly turned her camera back off again, looking at Jack with blank eyes, who came to her side instantly.

'Are you okay? You look like you've seen a ghost.'

Holly shook her head. 'Not a ghost ... but maybe a Christmas fairy,' she murmured quietly.

Suddenly, she laughed. Clapping a hand over her mouth, she laughed again and looked up at Jack, who was smiling at her apparent happiness. ‘Do you believe in fairies?’ she asked him. ‘Or Christmas wishes?’

Jack looked sheepish. ‘Well, no ... but I did ...’ he flushed as red as his Santa hat. ‘I did make a wish recently,’ he admitted. ‘I was out with my niece and nephew at a wishing well and—’

‘What was the wish?’ Holly asked eagerly.

He flushed again. ‘That I might get another Christmas kiss from you.’

Holly laughed merrily, before tugging on Jack’s hat, pulling his face near to hers.

‘I think,’ she whispered softly, ‘that your wish will definitely come true.’

She kissed him and heard the jingle of a bell. And while it was probably the bell on her hat or his, Holly definitely knew that somewhere, a fairy was getting her wings.

** The End **

The Girl Upstairs

Sharon Ibbotson

Nick thought he might hate the girl upstairs.

He hadn't even seen her, not really. Just a few fleeting glimpses on the stairwell, a flash of honey hair, long fingers wrapped around the bannister.

But he heard her. He heard her all the time.

He'd been living in Paris for three months when she moved in. He was renting an apartment in the dixième arrondissement of the city, a pleasant enough place, close but not too close to the tourist centre. He worked by day and kept to himself by night, just the way he wanted it.

And then *she* moved in.

At first, he thought she might be the ideal neighbour. She arrived in mid-September with absolutely no disruption to his life. One day, there was an *appartement à louer* sign outside the building, and the next day it was gone. She must have swept the stairwell at one point, because the communal hall was suddenly cleaner. She kept an umbrella by the doorway, practical, black and sturdy, next to a floral pair of rain boots. The boots were a splash of colour that made him smile despite himself, and when she got home at night she picked up his mail, dropping it on her way up to the loft.

The ideal neighbour, until the day she suddenly wasn't.

It was early October when Nick realised that this woman mustn't ever sleep. Because he could hear her, all night, dancing upstairs.

He lay in bed every night, the pounding beat of her footsteps heavy above him. He tossed and turned, every thought disrupted by the *tap-tap-tap* coming from his ceiling. He covered his head with his pillow, trying to drown her out.

One night, his temper frayed with tiredness, he went upstairs and angrily rapped on her door. When she answered, her eyes widened in surprise, and she began talking to him in a rapid stream of French.

'Look, stop, I'm Australian,' he finally said, rubbing a hand along his tired face. 'I mean, *je suis Australien ...*'

'Oh,' she said, in a clipped British accent. 'Oh, you're Australian?'

'Yes.'

'Oh,' she said again, regarding him thoughtfully. 'I suppose you must still be on Australian time then?'

'What? No. I've been here three months.'

'Really?' she leaned against the doorway, 'Because it's two in the morning here, and some of us are trying to sleep.'

'*What*?' He exploded. 'I'm trying to sleep! You're the one keeping me awake!'

She stared at him blankly. 'Impossible.'

'You …' in the face of her calm demeanour, he found words difficult. 'You keep walking around – or dancing, or marching, or whatever it is you're doing – and the sound in my apartment ... it's so loud, and —'

'I've been in bed since 10 p.m.,' she told him, crossing her arms. The movement made her shirt ride high against her hips and Nick's eyes drifted down, taking in her long legs, tanned and smooth.

'Look,' he spluttered, bringing his eyes swiftly back up to hers. 'You don't have to lie. Just quit moving around at night. Let me get some sleep.'

'I'm not lying,' she spat. 'I'm a nanny. I'm on my feet twelve hours a day taking care of two small girls. I need sleep if I'm going to function. And right now, you're interrupting that time.'

'I need sleep too,' he said. 'I'm working on a novel—'

‘A novel?’ she interrupted. ‘Does your novel need breakfast at 7.30 in the morning? Or dropping off at school at 8.45?’

‘No,’ he replied slowly. ‘But …’

‘Well then, you’ll forgive me if I cut short this charming “say hello to the new neighbour” routine you’ve got going and get back to bed.’

‘All I ask is that you keep it down, please,’ he begged.

‘I was never keeping it up to begin with.’ She shrugged. ‘Talk to the landlord, if you think I’m a problem.’

Nick grimaced. She was a problem alright. ‘Look, I came up here thinking we could solve this like reasonable adults.’ He sneered at her. ‘Clearly I was mistaken.’

‘Clearly,’ she replied. She licked her lips – lips that Nick suddenly could not stop looking at – and regarded him thoughtfully. ‘Goodnight, *Australien.*’

‘No, wait—’ Nick started to protest, but the woman firmly closed the door in his face.

She didn’t bring up his mail after that. And she stopped sweeping the hallway, so that when winter arrived in full force there was a difficult build-up of mud and leaves outside his door. And the noise didn’t improve – if anything, she got louder, and for longer periods of time.

By Christmas, Nick was ready to kill her. If the cold didn't first, that was.

Because Paris in winter, he quickly learned, was incredibly unappealing. He had his heating set to full blast and he bought extra layers to keep warm when the snow started to fall in earnest. A cold snap coming over from Russia was blanketing Western Europe in thick layers of snow and ice, and half a continent practically shut down. Trains stopped running, airports closed, buses were non-existent. Nick made a hazardous run to a supermarket to stock up on essentials before hunkering down to wait out the storm.

On Christmas Eve, he heard a pitiful knock on his door.

It was her.

She stood before him, her teeth chattering, her lips nearly blue. She was wrapped in a coarse blanket, clutching two pot plants, and he stared at her for a moment, uncertain of what to do or say.

'Please help me,' she whimpered. 'Please,' she said again. 'My plants ...'

He ushered her into the warmth of his apartment, taking the plants from her frozen hands and putting them on his desk.

'What's going on?' he asked her gently. It was Christmas, and not the time to reignite their feud.

'My heating's gone,' she told him. 'Broken, I think. It's Christmas Eve, and they can't send out a serviceman to repair the boiler until after the holidays.'

For a moment, they sat in silence. The woman was shaking still, her skin almost translucent. Nick jumped to his feet. 'I should make you some coffee.'

'I don't want to be too much trouble!' she protested, but he shook his head.

'I was going to have some anyway,' he assured her. 'It's no trouble.'

By the time he pressed a hot cup into her hands, she looked warmer. She sipped at it gratefully, and he noted with satisfaction how the blue was fading from her lips. Lips that, once again, he couldn't stop looking at.

'Look,' she said suddenly, not looking at him. 'I can cope with the cold. I'm British, coping with the cold is my birth right. But I have some plants upstairs that can't cope with the cold. And you would be doing me an absolute favour if I could leave them with you until my heating is fixed.'

Nick stared at her. 'Plants?'

'Yes.' She finally met his eyes. 'You know, green, leafy things that grow in dirt?'

'I think I've heard of them.' Nick nodded.

She almost smiled. 'Can I bring them here? I promise, you won't have to do anything with them, in fact …' She swallowed. 'I would respectfully ask you not to touch them. You don't look like the houseplant type.'

'Hey, I have a houseplant,' he replied.

She looked surprised. 'Really?'

'Yes. It came with the apartment. Wait, hang on …' He went into his bedroom and gingerly picked up his houseplant, proudly carrying it back through to the living room. 'See? I put it in the sun and water it occasionally, but it's doing really well.'

'It's plastic,' the girl stated bluntly.

'What? No, look, it's in dirt and—'

'It's plastic,' she said again. 'The dirt is a feature, as is the stem. But the leaves aren't real.'

They both stared at the plant – the fake plant – in his hands.

'You've been watering a plastic plant, *Australien*?'

Nick put the plant down. 'So it would seem.'

She burst into laughter. She covered her face, trying to hide her amusement, but the laughs trickled out, until even the red-faced Nick was smiling.

'So, I'm not green-fingered.' He shrugged eventually, still smiling.

'No,' she agreed, also smiling. She was pretty, Nick decided. Gorgeous in fact, all fine lines and soft eyes.

Suddenly, she blushed. 'What's your name, *Australien*?' she asked softly.

'Nick,' he said, his voice lower and huskier than he intended.

She nodded. 'I'm Alice.'

'Alice,' he repeated back to her, liking the sound.

'Nick,' she said, trying his own name out, almost as though tasting it.

Later, he helped Alice move her plants to his apartment. Her place was freezing.

'You can't stay here,' he said, absolutely aghast.

'It's Christmas. I've nowhere else to go.'

'You could stay with me,' he offered.

She looked at him warily.

'Not … I mean.' His face was hot, his words flustered, 'I mean, I have a couch – a sofa – you could sleep on that. I mean, I could sleep on that, and you could stay in my bed – I mean, in the bed, and …'

Alice looked down. 'I couldn't trouble you like that,' she replied. 'But thank you.'

Nick frowned. He couldn't countenance the thought of Alice sleeping here, in this icebox on Christmas Eve, while he was warm downstairs.

'Alice,' he beseeched.

She sighed, nodding slowly. 'Okay. Thank you, Nick.'

'It's nothing.' He looked away. 'It's Christmas.' He reached out to take a plant from her hand, ready to carry it downstairs. As he did so, his fingers brushed against hers and he felt a jolt in his stomach. He glanced at Alice. She was staring at their fingers, her eyes wide.

They both smiled.

In the morning, the snow was still coming down in thick rivulets, covering Paris in a thick, white blanket. Alice made coffee and warmed croissants in the kitchen, singing carols softly to herself. She started slightly when Nick cleared his throat, before smiling at him.

'Good morning,' she said. 'Coffee?'

He nodded, taking a cup from her hand. 'Thanks.'

'Did you sleep well?' she asked politely.

'Actually, yes,' he admitted. 'For once I did. You aren't so loud when you're down here, you know. No midnight dancing coming from my ceiling.'

She crossed her arms. 'I'm really not so loud,' she said, her forehead creased slightly. 'And trust me, I'm no dancer. Two left feet,' she added ruefully.

Nick shrugged. 'It's Christmas morning. It doesn't matter right now.'

'It does to me,' Alice replied. 'I just don't understand … all I ever do at night is eat, water my plants, flick on my heating and go to bed … I don't do anything that—'

'Wait,' Nick interrupted. 'You put on your heating? Every night?'

'From ten till five,' she clarified.

'You mean your heating which is currently broken?' Nick asked, unable to help a grin from spreading across his face.

Alice's mouth opened suddenly. 'The pipes,' she whispered. 'It's my pipes, isn't it?'

Nick nodded. 'I think it might be.'

'Oh, I'm so sorry, Nick. I'll get the landlord to—'

Nick held up his hand. 'Alice, I told you. It's Christmas morning. It doesn't matter right now.'

'You're right.' She paused, smiling at him. 'Merry Christmas, *Australien.*'

He smiled back. 'Merry Christmas, Alice.'

For a moment, they stood in silence, looking at each other. Abruptly, Alice blushed, before looking away. 'I'm going to use your shower, if that's okay?'

He nodded, watching her leave the kitchen, her hair brushing softly against her shoulders.

He had a feeling it was going to be a good Christmas. The apartment was warm, the air heavy with the smell of cinnamon and freshly watered plants. Paris through his window was quiet, the snow still falling across the city.

And Nick ...

Well, Nick thought he might just be in love with the girl upstairs.

* The End *

Find out more about Sharon Ibbotson and her novels here:

https://www.choc-lit.com/productcat/sharon-ibbotson/

Sharon's novels include: Hanukkah at the Great Greenwich Ice Creamery, A Game of Desire & The Marked Lord

Perfect Match

Jan Brigden

The last place I expected to find myself on the coldest day of the year was perched on a plastic blue seat, four rows back from the front, in the noisiest, windiest end of our local team's football ground. We're not talking stiff breeze, here; these arctic gusts are rattling my back fillings. Hooray for my bobble hat.

I wouldn't mind, but I don't even like football. My older sister's the big fan; knows everything and never misses a home game. I'm here because she had a spare ticket. My brother-in-law would normally be sitting where I am, but he's in Prague this weekend on a stag do with three other of the match regulars, hence my invitation. My sister thought it might cheer me up: 'Oh come on, Clare. What else have you got to do this weekend? It's better than sitting indoors moping over jealous John Simmonds. I bet he hasn't spent the last six months living like a recluse.'

No, he's currently in Jamaica with his new girlfriend, I wanted to shout, but decided my sister loathed him enough already, without me fueling her rage.

Fully justified rage, I might add, given the way he dumped me.

I'd embarked on a fitness and weight loss drive after struggling to run for my bus one day, the breathlessness spurring me into action. Instead of encouraging me, my boyfriend morphed into a petulant whiner, pooh-poohing Pilates and criticising the gym I joined, convinced that my healthier eating plan, newfound confidence and slimmer figure must be for some other man's benefit.

No, John. I did it for ME, not for you.

The whole bruising episode left me floored. I initially said no to coming here today; my usual answer to most invitations I've received since my split with John, but then big sis played the emotional blackmail card, reminding me how I'd never actually been to see the team play, even though the young son of a good family friend of ours made his debut for them in midfield six months previously. 'He'll be our Captain one day, sis! You're the only one in the family who hasn't seen him play. He's brilliant.'

Well, I had no excuse really.

I glance up as some bloke in a beanie hat heads over. He has a mate in tow and seems to know most people in our section, judging by the warm greetings and hand-shakes. Must be a regular, although I can hear a few people saying 'long time no see' to him, so maybe not.

He looks pleasant enough. All dimples and laughter lines. Forty-ish, I reckon. Older than his mate, anyway. Or it could be his son, I suppose? He gives me a friendly nod of acknowledgement and sits beside me, a rolled up programme in one hand, the few mid-brown curls escaping his hat.

Not that I'm staring or anything …

I smile back at him, squinting against the might of another frosty blast that lifts and buffets my fringe into some weird oblong shape in the centre of my forehead that I casually re-shape with my fingers and tuck further under my hat.

His eyes widen. 'Bloody freezing, eh?'

I laugh. 'You can say that again.' We share another smile, his gaze still on me as I turn away at the feeling of my sister nudging my elbow.

'Lucky thing,' she says, all wide-eyed, with a sly head-tip towards my neighbour.

I'm about to reply to her but the woman in front of us claims her attention – a fellow-regular, I assume, hearing the two of them debating the team selection.

Next thing, a huge roar goes up. A song blares out from the stadium speakers that sets everyone off singing – the team anthem, obviously.

Soon the referee's blowing his whistle and the game's underway and the strangest thing is, instead of peeping at my watch every five minutes and feigning interest in a game I'm clueless about, I'm bouncing around in my seat, whooping and hollering and cheering on our talented family friend, oohing and ahhing at every slick pass or near miss, like a match veteran. My sister thinks it's hilarious. 'I knew you'd enjoy it,' she bellows over the din of the chanting fans.

No kidding.

When our team score a screamer in the forty-fourth minute, I'm out of my seat. As is Mr Beanie Hat. Cheering our heads off, we are.

'You stay there, I'll grab us some coffees,' says big sis, bounding off up the steps like a whippet at the half-time break. Mr Beanie Hat's friend shoots off too; same idea, I guess. I don't envy them the refreshments queue. Must be like the first day of the Harrods sale.

'Great match,' Mr Beanie Hat says to me, both of us standing simultaneously to stretch our legs.

‘Yes, let’s hope the second half is as good.’ I shiver against the force of another blustery onslaught. ‘A bit of sunshine wouldn’t go amiss.’

He blows on his hands, rubs them together. ‘Yes, typical. The first weekend in ages I’ve been able to come to a game and winter makes an appearance. My son’s friend couldn’t make it today, so I took his ticket.’

Hmmm ... so it’s father and son then ...

No wedding ring, though.

Not that it’s my business ...

‘I took my sister’s husband’s ticket,’ I say. ‘He’s at a stag do this weekend. This is the first match I’ve ever been to.’

‘That’s your sister with you, I take it?’

‘Yes. She’s a season ticket holder. They both are. I’ve never been into football myself … well, until today.’ I feel myself blush that he might think I mean because of his presence and go on to explain the family friend connection.

‘You must be impressed,’ he says. ‘He’s doing great.’

‘Yes. I just hope he stays grounded. Footballers’ reputations are shocking, aren’t they? Be dreadful if he turned out to be a flash, arrogant womaniser, chucking his cash around, like most of them you read about online.'

'Half of which is exaggerated. Not all of us are bad.'

Us?

I feel my face crumple in horror.

He turns away to relieve his approaching son of one of the two coffees he's carrying.

'There you go,' says my sister at that moment handing me my own.

I gawp at her. 'You never told me he was a footballer.'

She peeps past me at Beanie Hat and grins. 'You never gave me a chance. You've been too busy chatting to him. Why, is there a problem?'

'Oh, only me and my big mouth probably offending him and most of his profession.'

'Ex-profession,' says sis under her breath. 'His career was cut short in his twenties. Broke his leg in two places. Had about a dozen operations in total. Terrible, eh? I believe he still works for the club in some capacity, on the corporate side.'

I take a massive gulp of my coffee, wishing I could be fired from my seat like a canon-ball.

No doubt he's told his son what I said.

How embarrassing.

‘Hey, don’t worry about it. He’s still smiling so he can’t be that miffed,’ says sis, giving my hand a reassuring squeeze. ‘Drink up! Second half starts in a minute.’

I down my coffee as play resumes.

The match gallops on to the final whistle, but I’m so mortified about what I said, even the 4-0 victory doesn’t cheer me up.

We all stand in unison and shuffle off to join the dawdling queue bound for the various exits. If I don’t say something to Beanie Hat now, I’ll lose my nerve.

A gap appears so there's more room to manoeuvre as people veer off in different directions. I tell my sister to go on ahead and that I’ll meet her outside.

I stay on Beanie Hat’s tail, his son one step ahead of him, and lay a hand on his arm before they reach a set of steps. ‘Could I have a quick word before you go?’

His dark eyes, full of intrigue, meet mine. ‘Sure.’

He signals to his son that he’ll catch him up and leads me into a sheltered recess away from the noisy zig-zagging throng, most of whom are still belting out their victory song.

And then the singing fades and he’s looking at me, waiting for me to speak. My heart rate spirals upwards. 'I'm so sorry if I insulted you,' I bluster. 'I'm not normally that judgemental, I'm just a bit crabby with people lately. I felt terrible when my sister told me about your injury.'

'Don't worry,' he says, kindness reflected in both his voice and expression. 'To be honest, some footballers are exactly how you described. I should know. My now ex-wife ran off with one.'

'Not when you were injured, I hope?'

'No, a week after I was forced to retire. Their relationship lasted about six months from memory.'

My mouth sags open. 'Gosh, how awful.'

'At the time, yes, but the signs had been there during my rehabilitation, people questioning her lack of support …' he sighs '... all water under the bridge as they say. She remarried a while back. Things are amicable between us now which helps as far as Luke is concerned.' He gestures in the general direction the teenager last strolled.

'My sister says you still work in football,' I say, my confidence bolstered by his openness with me.

'Yes, I run health and well-being workshops in one of the suites here at the stadium. My own experience taught me how important it is to have that support and encouragement when life enforces change on you, how isolating it can be when you're going through stuff, but equally how rewarding it can be to learn new things about yourself and what you're capable of. I mainly work with players with long-term injuries or addictions, ex-players, managers, coaches. Most weekends we open it up to the general public, as the advice and suggestions we share can be adapted to anyone going through a tough situation, whether it be personal, career-related or anything. We don't pressure people to talk straight away but hope they might feel comfortable enough to open up and share their experiences at some point.'

'Sounds wonderful,' I say a little too longingly, with a small gulp. 'I can definitely relate to it.'

He stares at me as if tapping in to my soul. 'Come along if you like, learn a bit more about what we do. You don't have to participate if you don't want to, you could come as my guest. I promise you the buffet lunch afterwards is a triumph. Assuming you don't mind sharing a table with me, that is?' He grins at me, reaches into his coat pocket, pulls out a card and hands it to me. 'Have a think about it.'

I stare down at it, reading his name and contact information. *Adam Willis – senior well-being facilitator.*

‘Thank you, Adam. I will.’ I smile up at him. ‘Lovely to meet you. I’m Clare.’

‘Lovely to meet you too, Clare. I hope to see you again soon.’

We share a smile and wave each other off, him in the direction of his waiting son, me towards my sister who, instead of meeting me outside, is standing halfway up a nearby stairwell, beaming at me.

‘That looked like a very cosy chat,’ she says, linking arms with me. ‘Save the weather, it’s been a great day, I reckon. Fab result too. The perfect match for you to attend, sis.’

‘Absolutely,’ I say, beaming back at her. ‘The perfect match in every way.’

* The End *

Find out more about Jan Brigden and her novels here:

https://www.choc-lit.com/productcat/jan-brigden/

Jan’s novels include: *As Weekends Go & If I Ever Doubt You*

All I Want For Christmas

Angela Britnell

Vicky had worked as a hotel receptionist long enough to be used to odd requests, but occasionally one still caught her out. 'Let me run through your list one more time, Mrs Bunt, to make sure I've got it right. You want a picnic lunch ready tomorrow – that's Christmas Day – at eleven o'clock in the morning. A warm pasty, a bag of cheese and onion crisps, egg sandwiches on white bread, a slice of Battenberg cake and a thermos of milky tea.'

'You're spot on dear – and call me Lila.'

Most guests, and especially visiting Americans, couldn't get enough of The Boscawen's extravagant Christmas festivities but Lila had politely declined to join in any of the activities and now wanted to skip tomorrow's gourmet meal.

'It's okay, honey.' The corners of Lila's mouth turned up in a smile. 'Let's just say I'm not a Christmas person.'

'It's not a problem. We'll deliver the food to your room.' Vicky checked her records. 'If it's not raining the view from the Trelawny Suite over the gardens is sublime. You'll have a pleasant spot to enjoy your meal.'

'Oh, I'm not eatin' up there.' Lila's husky laughter filled the lobby. 'I need you to book me a taxi to go to Penlanow Beach. I would've walked but the weather forecast is lousy.'

The beach? Vicky struggled not to show her dismay. 'Of course.' She spotted the large, noisy Hendon family heading towards the bar and caught the flash of envy in Lila's bright blue eyes. 'I expect they're going to listen to the carol singers. The performance starts at six o'clock and we're serving mulled wine and mince pies.' Vicky hoped that might tempt her but Lila frowned.

'I'd prefer a bite of supper in my room tonight, if that's okay?'

'Of course. Will around seven o'clock work?'

'Sure, and I'm not fussy what it is. I'll let your wonderful chef surprise me.' Her eyes brightened. 'I've gotta say your food is outstanding. My memories of English cooking were shaped from my first trip here way back in the early '70s. Y'all hadn't heard about putting ice in drinks, everything was overcooked and the joke was on you if you asked for a decent salad dressing.'

‘Our head chef, Tristan, is amazing. We’re lucky to have him.’ Vicky hoped the other woman didn’t notice her warm cheeks. Even talking about the handsome chef turned her into a tongue-tied mess; more like a teenager with her first crush than a grown woman within shouting distance of forty. The staff gossip mill labelled him as single but a workaholic; the first to arrive in the kitchen every day and the last to leave. She guessed that, like her, he had little in the way of a private life to rush home for. ‘I’ll let the kitchen know about your supper,’ Vicky promised.

‘I reckon you should tell him in person.’ Lila gave her a cheeky wink and disappeared back up the stairs.

She mulled over whether to accept the challenge but spotted Paul the head waiter coming out from the dining room. ‘Could you take a message to chef, please? I can’t leave reception at the moment.’ Vicky handed over the note with Lila’s supper request. *Coward*, she thought to herself.

Lila examined the hot drinks tray. She’d no interest in Christmas spice tea bags or pumpkin latte granules so plumped for a mug of plain old-fashioned coffee. She shifted the dark red velvet armchair closer to the wide bay window and settled down to think. If Arnold was here he'd tell her off for interfering, before smiling and calling her a hopeless romantic. All the cute little receptionist needed was a nudge. And the chef? When Tristan came over to her table to ask if she'd enjoyed her breakfast this morning her old heart had fluttered in a good way. By the time her eyes drooped with tiredness she knew what to do.

'Mrs Bunt, I've brought your supper.'

A loud rap on the door and the timbre of a man's deep voice startled her awake.

'Come in.' She was surprised to see the head chef. 'Oh, aren't you a dear to bring it yourself?'

'It's no trouble. I'm happy to escape the madness for a few minutes.'

If she closed her eyes it was like listening to Arnold's soft Cornish accent all over again.

'I'll leave you to enjoy your supper and have your picnic ready on time in the morning.'

Lila almost confessed the truth behind her strange request, but in the end simply thanked him. Arnold was the only person to understand the reason behind her dislike of the festive season and never called it childish. That was why she was here now, to see through the plan they made but never got to enjoy together.

Vicky wriggled her sore toes. It'd been stupid to wear her new strappy gold shoes today, but they suited the red dress she'd chosen to replace her everyday black and white uniform so vanity had won out.

'Here you go – one pasty picnic for our American guest.' Tristan emerged from the back and hefted a small wicker basket up on the desk.

'Oh, thank you ... and Happy Christmas.'

'Same to you.'

Normally their conversations lasted all of a few seconds before he hurried off back to work, but today he appeared to be studying her.

'Red suits you.' His face was hot from working in the kitchen but now he flushed a deeper shade of crimson. 'Sorry.'

'What for?'

'Your boyfriend might not appreciate me making personal comments.'

'Boyfriend?' Since she'd moved back to Cornwall her only dates were with Netflix and frozen ready meals.

He pushed away a strand of thick, white-blond hair from his face and looked awkward. 'The man who sometimes gives you a lift after work.'

A warm feeling ran through Vicky. Her cousin, Harry, worked in Mevagissey and often drove her home if he happened to be passing when she got off her shift. 'Oh, that's nothing serious.' She didn't consider the little white lie too out of line.

'Good. I—'

'Is that my picnic?' Lila emerged from the lift decked out in bright yellow waterproofs.

'Yes, and your taxi is outside.' Vicky forced herself to concentrate on the task at hand. 'You'll need your raincoat, I'm afraid.'

'A little bit of water never hurt anyone.'

Over the older woman's shoulder Tristan gave her a wry smile, and it took all her self-control to keep a straight face. It'd been tipping down all morning and showed no signs of letting up any time soon.

'Well I've got the first sitting of lunch to see to,' he said. 'Have a good day, ladies.'

Vicky gazed longingly after him.

'I must go now, dear, but I'd change out of those shoes if I was you or you'll pay the price when you're my age.'

She didn't bother to ask how the American guessed about her sore feet – the old lady was too shrewd by half. 'Enjoy your picnic.'

‘Oh, I will, don’t worry. I won’t stay gone for long in this weather.’

Lila disappeared with a cheery wave and Vicky went back to work, still wondering what it was Tristan didn’t finish saying to her.

Thick mist shrouded the beach and Lila carefully picked her way down the broad dark stones leading down to the sand. *Happy Birthday to me*, she thought. Her parents weren’t really to blame. She was born as the war was ending and there was no spare money for birthday celebrations, so it made sense to roll the two occasions into one. When Lila married and had her own family she’d made her daughters’ birthday parties as over-the-top and memorable as possible. The fact that neither Heidi nor Paula were December babies was no accident.

Today was supposed to be the first ever birthday totally about her. Arnold had squared it with their daughters that for Lila’s seventy-fifth he’d take her back to Cornwall where they met. On Christmas Day they’d recreate the picnic his mother made for their first date and, apart from leaving presents behind in Tennessee for the grandchildren, they’d do nothing to acknowledge Christmas.

But Arnold's heart condition caught up with him back in the spring, so here she was on her own. For two pins she'd ring the taxi driver now to whisk her off back to the warm, comfortable hotel.

Don't be daft, Lila love. Eat up your picnic, then have a bit of fun with those youngsters. Be careful, though. We don't want to frighten them too much.

Arnold's reprimand made her laugh and a new surge of mischief bubbled up. She would find a protected spot by the cliffs to eat her lunch and settle down to wait.

Vicky left Paul in charge of reception and headed to the kitchen for her overdue break. The second sitting of lunch was over, and there was nothing scheduled until the quiz at six o'clock followed by a light buffet supper.

'Would you like to join us?' Tristan called across. 'We're all taking a break. It's mainly leftovers from lunch, I'm afraid.'

'Don't apologise. All of your food is amazing.' Vicky caught a couple of the staff smirking at them.

'In return for that compliment you get the dubious privilege of sitting next to the head chef.' Tristan pulled out a chair, poured them both a glass of champagne and offered her a plate of delicious canapes. 'How did our intrepid American enjoy her picnic? I hope she didn't get washed away?'

She couldn't believe she'd forgotten all about Lila.

'What's wrong?'

'I've been busy,' she stammered. 'I didn't see her come back.'

'I'm sure she's fine.'

Vicky pushed her chair away. 'I'll go back out and check whether her key card's been used.'

'I'll come with you.'

They walked out together and the head waiter frowned at her from behind the reception desk. 'You haven't been long,' he said.

'I need you to tell me the last time Mrs Bunt in the Trelawny Suite was in her room.'

The answer confirmed her worst suspicions. Just before eleven o'clock this morning.

'We'll take my car,' Tristan said.

'But you're far too busy.'

'I'm not too busy for this … or you.'

Despite everything, she couldn't help smiling.

'I'll pop back to the kitchen to grab my keys and let Mandy know to take over. It's not a problem. Everything's organised for later.' He grinned down at her feet. 'You might want something less glamorous for the beach.'

'I'll change and come around the back to meet you,' Vicky said, and then quickly explained the situation to Paul.

She slipped on her sensible trainers and covered her dress with a sturdy rain jacket. Outside the kitchen door Tristan was waiting for her in his old green Land Rover, and she noticed the rain had dialled back to a soft drizzle. They drove the short distance to the beach and parked close to the steps.

'Could you dig out the torch in the glove compartment?' Tristan hopped out. 'I'll get the first aid kit and a blanket from the boot.'

Vicky grabbed the torch and joined him. 'We're going to look silly if she's fine.'

'She'll appreciate that we cared enough to check on her.'

They fruitlessly scanned the deserted beach.

'I used to play in some caves in the cliffs over there when I was a boy.' He pointed further down. 'She might have sheltered there to eat her picnic.'

'You grew up here?'

'For a while.' The shadows deepened in his face. 'After my mum died, Dad took us back to Bristol where he came from.'

'Oh, I'm sorry. I was born near Newquay but I left after school to work in London. When things … changed ... last year I needed to come back.' *Maybe one day she'd tell him the full story.*

They yelled Lila's name as they plodded across the wet sand.

'Shush, do you hear someone shouting?' Vicky took off running and Tristan caught up by the time she reached the entrance to the dark, narrow cave.

'Is someone out there?' Lila's trembling voice was unmistakeable. 'I need help.'

'We're coming.' She swept the wide beam of light around so they could see to press further inside.

'Oh, thank heavens. Am I glad to see you two?' Lila was sprawled on the ground and smiling weakly up at them. 'I sure am sorry. I've been a silly old woman.'

'We were worried when you didn't come back.' Tristan crouched down by her.

'That was the plan.' She looked sheepish. 'My Arnold said I could never resist a bit of drama, but I didn't mean to go this far. I tried to hide further back in the cave because I didn't want you to find me too easily, but I tripped and couldn't get back up.'

What on earth was she talking about? Vicky thought. 'Should we call for an ambulance in case you've broken something?'

'For heaven's sake, just get me off this wet sand or I'll have pneumonia tomorrow. I'm pretty sure I've only sprained my ankle.'

Between them they lifted her to her feet and wrapped the thick blanket around Lila's shoulders.

'We'll get a doctor to check you out at the hotel.' Vicky tried to look stern. 'And we'll expect a proper explanation later.'

Lila was aware she should be contrite, but she kept her counsel until the doctor left her with a bandaged up ankle and orders to rest. Vicky and Tristan's eyes widened when she explained about her matchmaking attempt.

'You hurt yourself on purpose to lure us there together?'

The receptionist clearly thought she was crazy and maybe she was.

'What if we hadn't come or you'd seriously hurt yourself?'

‘You were only supposed to catch me sleeping and we’d all be a bit embarrassed. Nothing more.’

‘All’s well that ends well. That’s the most important thing.’ Tristan gave her a kind smile and she hoped that meant she’d been forgiven. ‘I need to leave for a few minutes and get something from the kitchen. Vicky, why don’t you put the kettle on and make us all a hot drink? Black coffee for me, please.’

The young woman wasn’t as easily mollified and ticked her off again when they were alone. Then they heard a light knocking.

‘Can you open the door, please? I’ve got my hands full.’

Lila’s hand flew to her mouth when Vicky pulled back the door and there was the head chef holding a large pink cake topped with lighted candles. He started to sing ‘Happy Birthday’ and Vicky joined in, although she was clearly puzzled.

‘Blow out the candles and make a wish.’ He held the cake in front of her.

‘How did you know? You’re far too clever, young man.’

‘Am I the only one out of the loop here?’ Vicky asked. ‘It’s your birthday? On Christmas Day?’

‘Our dear friend here is seventy-five today,’ Tristan explained. ‘Her daughters contacted the hotel and ordered this cake.’

‘It’s the worst day to be born,’ Lila complained. ‘You never get a party and everyone thinks it’s okay to lump your presents together.’

‘Well, if it’s any consolation my birthday is on New Year’s Eve.’ Tristan chuckled. ‘It’s okay when you’re young, but later everyone’s too busy partying to celebrate your birthday. And don’t blame your daughters because they’re only following Arnold’s instructions.’

Tears stung her eyes.

Oh Lila, my love, enjoy it for me. Arnold’s gentle voice in her head put her straight.

‘Go on then, cut me a slice.’ Lila shrugged. ‘The two of you had better join me because it won’t be a party on my own, and I’m seventy-five years overdue one of those.’

* The End *

Find out more about Angela Britnell and her novels here:

https://www.choc-lit.com/productcat/angela-britnell/

Angela's novels include: *Christmas at Moonshine Hollow, A Summer to Remember in Herring Bay, New Year New Guy, Christmas at Little Penhaven, One Summer in Little Penhaven, Christmas at Black Cherry Retreat, Here Comes the Best Man, You're The One That I Want, Love Me for a Reason, The Wedding Reject Table, Celtic Love Knot, What Happens in Nashville & Sugar & Spice.*

Worse Than Shortbread

Ella Cook

'I know you're still new to the village, but you really should think about making more of an effort to join in.' Sylvia's neighbour chided her gently over their shared hedge. 'You've been here for months, but we hardly ever see you except for at the school gates.'

'I know, Julie.' Sylvia sighed as she watched the only friend she'd made since moving to the village. Julie moved quickly, clipping errant leaves with sharp, efficient movement. To Sylvia, the hedge already looked pristine, yet Julie still found leaves to remove. Perhaps, as she was a professional florist, she saw things that others missed.

'So what's stopping you?' She paused between snips.

'Nothing really,' Sylvia admitted. 'It's just that everything is so different here. It's so much greener, and quieter. I love it, but to be honest I miss the city's noise, the hustle and bustle. And being able to pop to the coffee shop when I want a decent caffeine hit and lemon poppy seed muffin.'

‘Well, there’s the coffee mornings in the village hall. But I think the only muffins you’ll get there will be toasted and come with butter.’

‘I know.’ Sylvia laughed. ‘It’s lovely here. I’m so glad I found this little cottage – I hadn’t thought that I’d be able to afford anything this nice for me and my son.’

‘Do I hear a “but” coming?’ Julie asked gently.

Sylvia nodded slowly. ‘But I just don’t really feel like I fit in here. James seems to like his new school well enough, but I’ve not really made any friends. Apart from you, of course.’

‘Which is why I keep nagging you to join in more,’ Julie argued reasonably.

‘It’s not like I don’t try,’ Sylvia complained. ‘I did get involved with the church coffee and cake morning.’

‘Yes, you did. And it was a really … memorable ... cake.’ Julie winced.

‘It was *supposed* to be a salted caramel sponge.’

‘It was definitely salty. No one could argue with that.’ Julie shook her head. ‘And then there was the shortbread you made for harvest festival.’

‘I did offer to pay for Mr Malone’s visit to the dentist.’ Sylvia still felt bad whenever she thought about the look of pain on the older man's face. 'Baking just isn't really my thing.'

'I won't argue with you on that. Especially as I've tried your rock cakes.' She pulled a face. 'They definitely live up to their name! But I might have the solution. There's a lot of people getting together at the weekend to decorate the village hall for Christmas. Some people bring food, and it usually ends up being a bit of a party. We're going to need loads of branches and foliage and pinecones and things.'

'Like holly and stuff?' Sylvia was sceptical.

'Exactly.' Julie nodded encouragingly. 'You can't go wrong with holly and ivy. And I'm sure your son would love it. My kids have been talking about it for weeks already. I'm going to bring all my floristry sprays and glitter in the afternoon after I close up my shop. It'll be lovely. Please say you'll try to come?'

'Alright, I'll do my best,' Sylvia promised, already thinking that gathering a few pinecones and some holly sounded a lot safer than being asked to bake anything.

So, early that Saturday, Sylvia bundled her James up in a hat, scarf and gloves against the cold and, ignoring his grumbles, headed to the nature reserve and woodlands that bordered the village.

'Why are we doing this again?' he complained, his breath puffing into clouds in the air around them. 'It's cold, and my friends are all gaming online. I'm missing a major quest.'

'We're doing this because it's a village tradition, and it'll do us both good to make some more friends.'

'I've got friends.' He glowered. 'They're waiting for me online.'

'And I'm sure they'll be there this afternoon. Or tomorrow. It'll be nice to get to know more people in the village.' She caught sight of his mutinous glare and softened her approach. 'Look, this is important to me. It hasn't been as easy for me to make friends as it has for you. I really do want to get to know some more people locally. Please?'

She smiled as her son bent down to scoop up some pinecones. 'Will these do?'

'Yes. They'd be perfect.'

'Cool. This should be easy then. Definitely better than you trying to bake again. I still haven't forgotten the gingerbread.'

Sylvia rolled her eyes and started scooping up the autumn flotsam and stuffing it into their carrier bags.

Golden acorns, russet conkers and leaves in every shade of red and amber were added to pinecones and spiky sprigs of holly speckled with bright red berries. Even vines of pretty red and yellow leaves were pulled down and added to their haul, tugged down by gloved fingers and stuffed into bags.

By the time they reached the village hall, their carrier bags were overflowing, and Sylvia proudly emptied them onto the tarpaulins in the middle of the hall.

'Right everyone,' one of the other mothers clapped her hands together brusquely while Sylvia tried to remember her name. 'Julie's been delayed, so we'll be without our florist until after lunch. But we've got plenty of willing hands here, and lots of lovely materials to work with, so let's crack on.'

Sylvia picked up a few pinecones and leaves and tried to follow the nimble fingers of another helper. It took her a few attempts, but eventually she managed to twist them together in a way that could be described as vaguely decorative. Determined that this event wouldn't turn into a debacle like her baking efforts, she picked up another collection of leaves and berries and began twisting them into pretty patterns, each grouping looking slightly less lopsided than the previous.

After a couple of hours, Sylvia flexed her fingers and stared proudly at her table. Yes, some of her decorations were a little stickier than ideal, but when they dried they'd look pretty. She scratched her arm absent-mindedly as she surveyed her handiwork. Maybe she'd join the village decorating committees and become one of their star designers. She could just see herself decorating the village hall for social events, looking humble while people praised her floral prowess.

She waved cheerfully as Julie staggered into the hall and dumped large bags on the table next to her. 'Hey, what do you think of my handiwork?' She yanked her sleeve up to itch at the red patch forming there.

'They're really pretty. Sure you haven't done this before?' Her eyes narrowed in concern as she stared at her friend's arm. 'Nasty rash you've got. Are you alright?'

'Probably just the wool jumper.' Sylvia shrugged the concern away while making a mental note to find a good cause to donate the offending garment to. Or an excuse to cut it into rags.

‘Julie!’ Bossy Mum called her. ‘Did you bring your glitter spray? Come see what we’ve been up to.’

Julie followed her around the hall obediently, oohing and aahing suitably until she reached the main podium, draped and dressed in Sylvia’s red and gold vines. Her face paled as she pulled a tissue out of her pocket and used it to examine a few of the leaves.

‘Oh no … Sylvia.’

‘What, what’s the matter?’

‘It’s not your jumper. This is toxicodendron radicans.’

Sylvia shrugged, not understanding.

‘Oh honey, this is even worse than your shortbread.’ Julie shook her head as the other helpers started to scratch and whisper. ‘You’ve given us all poison ivy.’

** The End **

Find out more about Ella Cook and her novel here: https://www.rubyfiction.com/productcat/ella-cook/

Ella’s novel: *Beyond Grey*

A Christmas Crisis

Kirsty Ferry

There's a chocolate short in my advent calendar.

Now, I know that it's maybe a bit early to realise that, because it's only the twelfth of December.

However, Christmas is a busy time of year, and I think it's only right if I take some pressure off myself by eating *two* advent calendar chocolates each day, rather than one. That gives me the second half of December to concentrate on things like giant tins of Quality Street (I have to sort them out, so my Dad gets the coconut eclairs delivered to him in good time for Christmas. Coconut eclairs are the most vile multi-pack chocolate ever invented, but Dad seems to like them, and it also frees up the strawberry cremes in their own tin for my mum, so it's win-win) and big tubs of Heroes (my favourites are the Dairy Milk chocolate chunks, and they're ever so nice with a cup of tea on an evening).

I treated myself to an artisan advent calendar this year from the chocolatier in one of those super-high-end shops I pass on my way to work. It's heaven in a shop, seriously. It is called "Chocolate Heaven" actually, so the clue's in the name, as they say.

Regardless, Easter has me pressing my nose to the window and drooling over the huge caramel-chocolate eggs, sprinkled with edible glitter dust; Halloween has me dribbling over the chocolate slab version of pumpkin spice lattes, and Christmas – well. Christmas. What can I say? Heaven, with Belgian chocolate holly berries on it.

Also, "They Know Me There", which is always a bit of an ominous phrase, because it implies that you could be known for a good reason or a bad reason. I hope I'm known for a good reason.

More than likely it's because I'm in there at least once a week buying a selection of delicacies to see me through the weekend. It's particularly nice at this time of year, because they make all the chocolatey treats on the premises, and it smells even more like Willy Wonka's Chocolate Factory. Obviously, I've never been to Willy Wonka's Chocolate Factory, but it's my favourite film, and my favourite childhood book. I'm called Violet, so of course I always identified with Violet Beaureagarde, but I can promise I'm an altogether nicer person than she is.

Anyway, I digress. The smell of winter spices and warm, melted chocolate and cream and spun sugar has me heading there like a magnet at this time of year.

Okay – so maybe I go *twice* a week at Christmas time, but who's counting?

Well, I say that, but clearly someone is, because Ben, the chocolatier who owns the place and works his magic behind the scenes, is on first name terms with me.

'Hey, Violet! You were only in two days ago. Everything okay?' He greets me with a big smile. I melt a bit, like a piece of Galaxy left in the sun too long. He's perfectly suited to his job; dark chocolate-brown eyes and hair the colour of giant chocolate buttons. I mean, what's not to like? He smells good too – just like his shop. I noticed this as he came out from behind the Counter of Dreams (yes, I'd love to work there) and helped me choose which chocolates I wanted in my calendar. I swear I saw him put all the chocolatey treats behind the little windows in the calendar – although I must confess, his back was to me while he did that so I had plenty of time to admire his denim-clad bum and close-fitting black T-shirt – which makes it all the more odd that one chocolatey treat is missing.

And it's the chocolatey treat that *should* be behind the window of the 24th. Christmas Eve. Technically, the biggest and best chocolate should have been in there, and that's how I had planned it.

Imagine my disappointment.

'No, Ben, actually everything is *not* okay.' I pull a sad face which makes him laugh. 'I'm a chocolate short of an advent calendar.'

That makes him burst out laughing. 'What, like a sandwich short of a picnic?' he teases.

'No!' I laugh. 'I truly mean I'm a chocolate short of an advent calendar. Number twenty-four. Christmas Eve. It's not there.'

'So may I ask why on the—' he checks his watch mock-seriously '—twelfth of December, this has come to your attention?'

I blush. *I'm going to have to confess, aren't I?* 'I ... um ... ate them. I wanted to get through it quickly so I had more time before Christmas to ... um ...' I shrug helplessly. 'Eat more chocolate?'

I feel myself flush a bit more and he blinks comically. 'Okay. Well, which type of chocolate is missing?'

'My favourite.'

'The violet crème?'

'Yes.' I nod. *Oh, come on, I had to love that one the best, didn't I, with a name like mine?*

‘I see. Violet, as you’re probably one of my best customers, I’m prepared to overlook the fact that all my fabulous creations have been scoffed before their time, and I trust you, so I’ll even offer to replace the violet crème for you. In fact.’ He ducks down behind the counter and comes up with a little gold gift-wrapped box. ‘Here’s one I prepared earlier.’

He grins at me and I laugh. ‘Thanks, Ben.’

‘Go on, you may as well open it now,’ he says. ‘I know you’re going to as soon as you leave the shop anyway.’

‘True, true.’ He’s not wrong.

Carefully, I untie the ribbon and open the tiny box. Inside, there is indeed a violet crème, all rich and delicious looking, with a real crystallised violet flower on top. Scrumptious.

‘Hang on a mo,’ I say, as I lift the chocolate out. ‘There’s something else in here?’

‘Is there?’ Ben looks surprised and leans over the counter to have a look. *Yep, he smells just as divine as always.*

‘It’s a gift card.’

‘Really?’

‘Yes. Oh!’ I look at him, baffled. ‘It’s got my name on it.’

‘Has it?’

‘Yes.’

‘Interesting. Why don’t you open it?’ he asks, and I look at him quickly. He’s a little bit flushed in the cheeks now and, as our eyes lock, he turns a more rosy colour. My heart starts beating a little louder and a little faster, and I find it hard to tear my gaze away from his. ‘Might as well,’ I say, and my voice is suddenly high-pitched and wobbly. I try to make a joke. ‘Might be a Golden Ticket.’

‘Might be.’

I open the envelope and gasp. It is indeed a Golden Ticket. I turn it over, and it says:

Violet Hargreaves. Please accept this ticket to an exclusive Chocolate Heaven Christmas Experience next Saturday. You will have a session of Festive Chocolate Making with Ben Foster, followed by an Elite Chocolate Tasting Event, and drinks afterwards at a location of your choosing. All you have to do to accept this gift, is say “yes”. P.S. Note there is no date quoted for “Saturday”. I wasn’t sure how long it would take you to finish your advent calendar.

I look up at Ben with a huge smile on my face, and it seems he's a tad nervous but also a little hopeful.

'Well?' he asks.

'Yes please – with jingle bells on,' I say.

And then, I break the chocolate in half and share it with him.

It *is* almost Christmas, after all.

** The End **

Find out more about Kirsty Ferry and her novels here: https://www.choc-lit.com/productcat/kirsty-ferry/

Kirsty's novels include: Holly's Christmas Secret, Lily's Secret, It Started with a Giggle, Christmas on the Isle of Skye, Jessie's Little Bookshop by the Sea, A Secret Rose, Spring at Taigh Fallon, A Christmas Secret, Watch for Me at Christmas, Summer at Carrick Park, Watch for Me by Twilight, Watch for Me by Candlelight, Every Witch Way, Watch for Me by Moonlight, A Little Bit of Christmas Magic, The Girl in the Photograph, The Girl in the Painting & Some Veil Did Fall .

Messages in the Snow
Morton S. Gray

There was a message in the snow just outside her garden gate. Jessica stepped out to read it as the snowflakes continued to fall.

You're lovely, was framed in a heart.

How wonderful for someone having such a sweet message drawn for them in the snow, she thought, lamenting the fact that she had no one special in her own life to do such a thing.

Later, when she returned home after work, there was a different message in the snow heart just outside of her gate. This one said, *I've always loved you.* It made Jessica smile, and she hoped the person it was intended for was happy too.

She was meeting a friend at the pub for a drink that evening and couldn't help but stop to see if the message had changed again. This time *Remember me* was carved carefully in the middle of the snow heart.

Jessica told Alison about the mystery messages when she'd ordered their gin and tonics, but Alison had a very different take on the snow notes.

'You haven't got a stalker, have you?'

‘A stalker?’ Jessica was genuinely astounded. ‘But I don’t think the messages were for me at all.’

‘You did say they were right outside of your garden gate though?’ Alison now had her hand on Jessica’s arm and a concerned look on her face.

‘I’ve not seen anyone lurking around outside. I’m sure it’s nothing creepy.’

‘Well, either way, there’s no way I’m letting you walk home on your own tonight. I’ll have to see you safely locked behind your front door , or I won’t be able to sleep.’

‘I rcally don’t think it’s anything to worry about!’

The friends were joined by other acquaintances then, but despite looking forward to the evening, Alison’s words began to play on her mind and Jessica found herself looking around the pub to see if anyone could possibly be watching her. No one appeared to be, but the worm of doubt began to grow.

By the time the friends left the pub, it had been raining and the snow had almost all melted away. Alison insisted on walking Jessica home and Jessica, by now a little fearful despite her earlier doubts, was grateful.

‘There won’t be any messages now, as there’s no snow to write them in,’ Jessica said brightly, more for her own benefit than for Alison.

But as they approached Jessica’s house, there was an obvious heart shape outlined in pebbles on the pavement outside of her front gate, illuminated by the nearby street lamp.

‘Look, there *is* another message.’ Alison grabbed her hand and towed her over to the pebble heart. Jessica didn’t really want to look, and in the end she didn’t have to as Alison read the words aloud.

‘It says “Love me again”. Are you sure you’ve no idea who could be doing this?’

‘We still don’t know they’re even for me, do we?’

‘Durr. I think the fact they are right outside your garden gate gives us a clue.’

‘Well, I’ve absolutely no idea. You know that my love life is totally non-existent ... has been for years.’

‘It must be someone who’s come home to Borteen for Christmas.’

‘Have you turned into an amateur detective all of a sudden?’ teased Jessica.

After her friend had gone home, making her promise to ring her straight away if she was at all concerned, Jessica sat in her lounge, cradling a hot chocolate, her ears alert for any sounds outside and her brain working overtime on who could possibly be leaving her those messages.

Her love life had been a desert for years, ever since the teenage love of her life, Guy Sallis, had emigrated with his family to America six years before. They'd parted as friends but had decided to go their separate ways, rather than trying to carry on a long-distance relationship. Guy was keen to embrace his new life in California and, although she was extremely sad about him leaving, Jessica hadn't wanted to leave England or hcr parents. As far as she was aware she'd not attracted the interest of anyone else since Guy had gone, but maybe she was wrong.

A vision of the little old man who lived down the road came into her mind and then the shy, spotty greengrocer's assistant for some reason. If this speculation continued she'd be suspecting every male she came across of being her secret admirer.

Intriguingly, after the four messages, there were no more for several days, and Jessica began to think she'd imagined the whole thing. She met up with Alison on Saturday morning to watch the annual Santa fun run, which a couple of other friends were running in. They stood near the finish line chatting and sipping takeaway coffees, while they waited for the starting pistol to sound. The event wasn't really a race, but most of the participants in their red Santa outfits seemed to view it as such and took it very seriously as they careered down the road closed especially for the fun run.

Alison and Jessica stood back against a wall to avoid being knocked over by the runners, but Jessica was astounded as the Santa running in the lead made straight for her and handed her a bunch of red roses before running on and being swallowed up by the crowd of red Santas.

Alison wanted to go after the runner but risked being mowed down by the rest of the Santas, and Jessica only just managed to haul her back against the wall. She looked at the beautiful bunch of roses in her hands.

'Is there a card? A note?' asked Alison.

There wasn't anything attached to the flowers and the possibility of identifying the particular Santa who had given her the roses seemed remote in the throng of red suits and white beards now amassed at the finish line.

‘Well, one thing is for certain, you have an admirer,’ crowed Alison.

Jessica wasn’t sure whether to be pleased or alarmed. The whole incident had happened so quickly that she couldn’t remember anything about the person who had given her the flowers apart from the obvious Santa suit and white beard.

She always visited to her parents’ house at Saturday teatime, and she made her way over there after putting the roses in a vase at home. Today, her mother was strangely quiet, but her father seemed excited – perhaps to make up for her mother’s quietness, Jessica thought. He ambushed her almost as soon as she sat down. ‘Have you seen Guy?’

‘Guy? He’s in America, remember?’

‘No, he’s back.’ Her father winked and her mother shrugged.

Jessica felt her heart rate accelerate. ‘Back? Back in Borteen?’

‘Yes, he came to see us, wanted to know all about you, well, whether you were married, still in town, that sort of thing.’

‘Really?’ Her heart was now thumping. Could Guy possibly have left the mysterious messages and given her roses? Jessica sat at the dining table as tea was served even quieter than her mother had been, as she tried to figure out how she felt about the possibility. The messages had said, *You're lovely*, *I've always loved you*, *Remember me* and *Love me again*. It all seemed to fit. It *had* to be Guy.

Snow was falling again as she left her parents' house, and she pulled up her hood and walked home as quickly as possible. There was someone leaning on the wall by her garden gate – even through the snow, she could see the person was dressed as Santa, complete with a white beard. She should have felt fearful, should have turned back, but instead she found tears blurring her vision as she let this special Santa enfold her in his open arms.

'I'm home, and I know that I should have never left you behind.'

'Is that home just for the holidays, or home for good?' she asked, holding her breath for the answer.

'I'm home for good. I've taken a job in Sowden. I know I have no right to expect anything from you at all, but I've regretted us parting every day since we did. I didn't contact you because I thought I should give you the chance to find someone else, but your dad said that you haven't, and I have to admit my heart leapt when he said that. Do you think you can give us another chance? A proper go this time, rather than just a teenage fling?'

'Well, Santa, I think you've just given me the best Christmas present I'll ever get.'

Jessica pulled down Guy's cotton wool beard and sealed the deal with a Christmas kiss she hoped would lead to forever.

** The End **

Find out more about Morton S. Gray and her novels here:

https://www.choc-lit.com/productcat/morton-s-gray/

Morton's novels include: Christmas at the Little Beach Café, Sunny Days at the Beach, Christmas at Borteen Bay, The Truth Lies Buried & The Girl on the Beach.

Closet Cinderella

Gina Hollands

Eleanor surveyed the racks of gowns she'd hung out. She couldn't wait to dress this year's prom-goers. This was her third year of running her shop, Closet Cinderella, and she loved every second. Even though she hadn't managed to get to her own prom all those years ago, it didn't take away the joy of pairing girls with their dream dresses. She switched the sign to open and prepared for a busy day.

Eleanor was making herself a cup of tea in the back of the shop when she heard the doorbell chime. It must be her last appointment.

'Hello,' she said to the man and young girl, who appeared to be father and daughter. 'You must be Tamsin.'

As the girl was in the fitting room, trying on dresses, Eleanor struck up conversation with her father, unable to shake the feeling she knew him. Although he didn't have as much hair as she remembered, and was thicker around the waist, he was still handsome.

‘James?’ she exclaimed, as she realised who he was. James Hawkin had been her biggest crush throughout school. She’d hardly believed her luck when he’d invited her as his date to the school prom.

It was clear from his blank expression that he didn’t recognise her.

‘Eleanor Baines! Yes, of course,’ he said when she gave her name. ‘The last time I saw you, you agreed to be my date to the prom.’

So, he did remember.

She’d been devastated she couldn’t go to the prom. She’d been looking forward to it since her first day at school, had spent years planning her outfit – a gorgeous red, satin mermaid gown – but on the day, she’d fallen ill with a tummy bug. She’d cried for a week afterwards, especially when she heard that James had found a replacement date and begun a relationship.

‘I never saw you again after that,’ James said. ‘I suppose everyone went their separate ways after school – jobs, marriage, divorce ...’ He gave a wry smile that she took to mean he was separated.

She thought back to her college days studying fashion, and the years spent working, saving to open her own shop. It hadn't left a lot of time for relationships.

'It doesn't seem right that the lady who owns Closet Cinderella never did go to the ball,' said James as he paid for his daughter's dress. 'My firm's sponsoring the summer charity ball at The Royal Hotel next week. How about you come as one of our guests?'

Eleanor nearly dropped the bag she was handing over the counter. Was he actually inviting her out? It was a second chance at her dream – a date with James Hawkin and a chance to go to a real ball.

'It starts at seven,' he said with a wink, as he and Tamsin left the shop. 'See you there.'

All week, Eleanor planned her outfit. As luck would have it, she had a dress similar to the one she'd planned to wear for her prom in stock. She practised up-dos from YouTube tutorials and carefully selected shoes and jewellery. She thought it slightly odd that James hadn't offered to pick her up but was too excited by the time that the ball came around to give it much thought.

She arrived at the hotel to find everything as she'd imagined – guests in their finery, a glittering chandelier and a huge ballroom, edged with tables set for dinner. She spotted her name on the table plan and found her place.

James and a group of what Eleanor assumed to be his work colleagues were already seated.

'Eleanor, you made it!' James said, kissing her cheek and introducing her to the others.

She was disappointed to find she wasn't seated beside James, but Marvin and Rick, who were a couple and sat either side of her, were fantastic company.

She glanced over at James, but he seemed too preoccupied with the pretty woman next to him to notice. It became obvious to Eleanor from the way he flirted with the woman that he only had eyes for her and wasn't interested in Eleanor at all. Her heart sank. Why had she assumed he was asking her out on a date? He'd never said that, only that she should come along. She felt like an idiot and vowed once dinner was over to leave. It would mean missing the dancing – the part she'd been looking forward to – but she didn't want to feel any more of a fool than she already did.

After the coffee was served, she excused herself, planning on making a swift exit. The others had been friendly, but they wouldn't miss her. They had dispersed now, anyway, some heading for the bar, others for the dancefloor.

Just as she was walking out the door, she realised she'd forgotten her phone and returned to the ballroom to get it.

'Hey, Eleanor!' She turned to see Marvin on the dancefloor strutting his stuff to a seventies' number. 'Come join us?'

She made an excuse, but Marvin grabbed her hand and pulled her onto the floor to join him and Rick and the other party-goers.

Before she knew it, it was midnight, and she hadn't stopped dancing once. The music lifted her spirits and made her feel alive. She even kicked off her diamante shoes so she didn't get blisters.

Rick caught her looking at her watch. 'What's the matter? Your coach won't turn into a pumpkin, will it?'

She smiled. 'I don't care if it does,' she said. 'This Cinderella is staying till the bitter end.'

'Thata girl.' Rick grinned. He twirled her around as a new track started up.

It was two in the morning when the band called it a night and the lights came on – a sign for everyone to leave. Still on cloud nine from having had one of the best nights of her life, she went to the bar for a glass of water.

‘Thirsty?’ asked the barman as she downed her drink.

She laughed. ‘I haven’t stopped dancing all night. I’ve had a fabulous time.’

‘I know,’ he said, his dark eyes twinkling. ‘I noticed. It’s good to see someone not holding back for a change and just enjoying themselves.’

She was glad her cheeks were already red from exertion, so that he couldn’t tell she was blushing.

‘And you look beautiful, by the way. That’s a lovely dress.’

‘Thank you,’ she said, looking down at her gown. Then she remembered she wasn’t wearing her shoes. She turned around but could only see one by the edge of the dancefloor. ‘Oh! My shoe is missing.’

‘How about,’ said the barman, ‘if I find it, you come out on a date with me?’

She didn’t know what to say. He seemed nice, but she didn’t normally get asked out on dates. Then again, she didn’t normally spend all night dancing like no one was watching. Maybe it was about time she lived a little.

‘All right,’ she agreed with a smile. ‘I’d like that.’ Then she frowned. ‘But what if you don’t find it?’

He gave a cheeky smile, bent down behind the bar and emerged victorious, holding up her missing shoe. ‘This it, by any chance?’

She laughed, took it off him and popped it on her foot. ‘It fits, so it must be.’

‘Good.’ He grinned. ‘Then I guess that means we have a date?’

She grinned back. Once upon a time she would have been devastated that James Hawkin hadn’t shown any interest in her. But a lot had changed this evening, and she had a feeling tonight was only the beginning.

** The End **

Find out more about Gina Hollands and her novel here:

https://www.choc-lit.com/productcat/gina-hollands/

Gina’s novel: Little Village of Second Chances.

Christmas Day: A Moving Experience
Margaret James

'Miaow? Miaow! Miaow! Miaow!'

What the hell?

Polly kicked and fought her way out of a ghastly nightmare – a headless man in armour was sitting in her kitchen stuffing cornflakes down his neck – to find a furry rucksack on her face.

She pushed it off and scowled at it.

The black cat glared right back, its green eyes glittering in the murky dawn. 'Miaow!' it said again. It was clearly used to giving idiots the same message until they got the ... message.

'Who let you in here?' demanded Polly.

'Miaow,' the cat replied.

'You should increase your vocabulary,' Polly told it. 'Say supercalifragilisticexpialidocious.'

'Miaow,' the cat said haughtily, doing what it did best.

Deciding to move house on Christmas Eve was never going to be a brilliant plan, Polly had realised the previous evening as she'd listened to her fuel supplier WeDriveAllOurCustomersMad.com's nerve-shredding rendition of 'Jingle Bells' for the ten thousandth time.

Nobody was answering the twenty-four-hour phone lines, obviously. She'd suspected everyone at WeDriveAllOurCustomersMad HQ must be at the office party getting stoned.

Or drunk.

Or snogging in the toilets.

Or photocopying their bums.

This was the sort of thing that happened at the office parties she had known and hated while she'd worked for Mammoth Pharmaceuticals UK.

Oh, well – who needed electricity? She had a phone, a torch and an electric lamp. Out here in the wilds of Devon, there were probably glow-worms. The trouble was, she didn't know in which of half a zillion erratically-labelled boxes full of clothes, books, china and the stuff she needed for her brand new hand-made-jewellery business she might find a glass …

The decision to move from London to a cottage in the middle of nowhere had not been lightly taken. It had been insanely, ridiculously taken, and now Polly was regretting it.

There was no Sainsbury's for twenty miles.

The nearest Marks and Spencer was in Plymouth.

Apparently, a bus drove past the lane that led to her decrepit cottage once a fortnight. So, if her ancient Civic decided it was time for it to go to Honda heaven, she was going to be kind of stuck.

She'd have to get a shopping trolley.

Yes, a tartan one with squeaky wheels and an umbrella down the side, like grannies used.

No no no no no!

It was not until long after she had won the auction, signed the contract, and there was no getting out of this absurd development, that she had made the big mistake of Googling the history of the village.

Why hadn't she done this before, at the drooling-over-property-porn-online stage?

She blamed her condition.

She discovered her own cottage used to be an ale house. The local headless huntsman – headless because Elizabeth I had had his head chopped off after he'd seduced a maid-of-honour and unwisely flirted with Mary Queen of Scots – manifested regularly, stabling his stallion in her scullery and hanging round her kitchen, pouring pints of ghostly ale down his severed neck, apparently.

So was this why she'd got the place so cheap? She

thought it had to be. Who but an idiot would want to share a kitchen with a headless Tudor drunk?

She'd made herself a mug of Horlicks on the ancient camping stove that some kind, thoughtful angel had prompted her to pack somewhere accessible. She decided to ignore the orange mushrooms sprouting all along the skirting boards, the grey mould cobwebbing the ceilings, the suspicious green stuff growing in the kitchen sink. She'd gone to bed under a pile of coats, not bothering to get herself undressed.

She didn't want to freeze to death on her first night.

Or to be accosted by the huntsman while wearing pink pyjamas, if he was used to hitting on queens and maids-of-honour in their best Tudor bling.

Maybe, she'd thought hopefully, as she drifted into troubled slumber, things would look a little better in the light of morning – Christmas morning?

The cat was getting very insistent now, tapping on her nose with one extended, razor claw. So Polly got out of bed and went downstairs. She boiled some water on the camping stove, she had a wash, and then she went outside. There was a light powdering of snow. She could hear church bells ringing in the distance.

'Miaow!' the cat repeated, winding sinuously between her legs and trying to trip her up. Once back in the kitchen, she found a cardboard box she'd labelled 'tinned stuff' and opened a small can of tuna. 'Happy Christmas, cat,' she said. She wondered vaguely where it lived.

Right here, I guess, her other self replied. *The people who sold this ruin to you left their cat as well.*

The cat was not impressed by Christmas breakfast. It was sniffing at the tuna in a way that suggested it must be used to something rather posher than ordinary supermarket fare.

'Go and catch a mouse, then,' Polly told it, opening the kitchen door again.

It did as it was told.

Or at any rate it cleared off sharpish.

Christmas Day is probably good for miracles, she thought, as she crossed her fingers, tried her mobile – and, to her amazement, got a decent signal.

She checked her website. No orders for her jewellery yet, but surely they would come?

'Setting up a hand-made jewellery business in the third week of December – nice one, love,' her ex-fiancé, Rupert, had said sarcastically. 'No one gets their Christmas presents any time before the 21st, so you'll clean up. As for that ruin of a cottage you've just bought—'

So then they'd had the fight.

No way was Rupert going to move to rural Devon. He was an urban man, was Rupert, always had been, always would be. As for Polly, she was clearly crazy, according to him.

'Well, it takes a lunatic to know another lunatic,' Polly had snapped back at him. 'Anyone who works a twelve-to-fifteen-hour day, who never sees his friends, his parents or his own fiancée because he's far more interested in spreadsheets must be missing several screws.'

But now she wished so much that he was here.

She should have told him calmly she needed to get out of the Big Smoke, explained that she was suffocating in their glass-and-chrome apartment with its views of other tower blocks full of other glass-and-chrome apartments. She and the little one-to-be should breathe fresh country air, not everlasting petrol fumes.

Yes, she and Rupert should have talked about it. They should have tried to reach a compromise. She shouldn't have thrown away all her late mother's money on this ... this stupid folly.

She hadn't even seen it before she signed the paperwork.

What was she, an imbecile?

A baby brain?

Of course – and, if the scientists were right, her brain was getting smaller by the day, the hour, the minute.

A healthy walk, she thought, after she'd had a festive Christmas breakfast of dry cornflakes and a tuna sandwich made of crackers. The biscuits, not the crepe-and-tinsel things. She hadn't bought any crepe-and-tinsel things.

The black cat had come back from mousing or whatever. Now it pranced along beside her, stopping every now and then to rub its face on fence posts, leaving pretty paw prints in the snow.

She passed the ancient, grey stone church. But it was shut and silent and she supposed the service must be somewhere else today, which might explain the lack of any people in the streets.

Then, as she crossed the village green, she met a solitary woman. 'Merry Christmas,' said the woman.

'Merry Christmas,' Polly parroted.

'You've moved into Ivy Cottage, haven't you?'

‘Yes, I came last night.’

‘I saw your van go down the lane. The men, they didn’t stay long.’

‘They wanted to get back to London,’ Polly said. ‘Whose is this cat, do you know?’

‘What cat?’

‘This black one ... oh.’

The cat had disappeared.

There were no paw prints in the snow.

‘We don’t have no black cats in Rowtonstock,’ the woman said. ‘We don’t have any cats in this here village – never have and never will.’

‘So the people at Ivy Cottage didn’t have a cat?’

‘They had a big Alsatian, like a wolf. It would have eaten any cat alive.’

A nutcase, Polly thought. *Of course you have black cats in Rowtonstock – and white and grey and tabby ones, as well.*

But, come to think of it, she hadn’t seen any other cats while she was out. No other cats at all …

‘Do you have a shop round here?’ she asked. *Yes, something else she hadn’t thought to check.*

‘The nearest shop’s in Moretonhampstead. But it won’t be open Christmas Day.’

Cornflakes for Christmas dinner, then, thought

Polly miserably.

She walked across some fields then made her way back to the cottage, up the humpy, bumpy lane that would probably finish off the Honda pretty soon.

She must have walked for miles and miles, which might not have been wise in her condition …

As she arrived back in the village, the black cat reappeared and now it skittered merrily along, jumping from rut to frozen rut. Polly stooped to stroke it, deciding she wanted to make friends with it.

Also she wanted to find out if it was real.

But it didn't fancy being stroked. It skipped away before she had a chance to touch it.

Perhaps it was a ghost cat, after all?

But hadn't she woken up to find it sitting on her face?

Or had she imagined it?

When they reached the cottage, the cat danced straight inside.

The place was cold and gloomy, and by this time Polly felt so low and lonely that she couldn't summon up the energy to scream or have a fit, even when she saw the ghostly huntsman was sitting on her sofa, his head upon his lap.

'You can't stay here,' she told him sharply. 'No witches, warlocks, vampires, spooks allowed. I don't believe in them.'

'Hello, Polly,' said the huntsman, pushing his motorcycle helmet to one side and then emerging like a tortoise from a carapace of scarves and collars. 'I had to come. I had to see you.'

'How did you find this cottage? I didn't give you the address.'

'But you said it was in Rowtonstock. I thought, when I arrived, I'd ask around, that someone would be sure to know somebody new had come.'

'So, you weren't just following a star?'

'I was following you, and you're my star. My guiding light. I know that now. Polly, how are you, and how's the—'

'Oh, the baby's fine.'

'What a relief.'

'This cottage, though, it's far from fine. It's rotting.'

'Rot can soon be fixed.'

'It's haunted, too.'

'Yeah?' said Rupert. 'Great! It's on my bucket list to meet a genuine ghost and shake it by the hand – that's if it's got a hand – before I die.'

'You can start with this cat, then,' Polly told him. 'You can shake it by the paw.'

'I'm sorry?'

'It's a ghost. They don't have black cats in Rowtonstock. Apparently, they don't have cats at all. So this one can't be real.'

'Who told you there are no cats here?'

'A woman in the village.'

'Pink bobble hat, green wellies, purple coat?'

'Yes, that's the one. How did you know?'

'She was walking past the village school when I arrived. I asked her if she'd seen a newcomer, if she knew where you lived. But she said she couldn't stop and talk to me. She had to go straight home to feed her geese and porcupine.'

'She has a porcupine?'

'Yes, so she said. She seemed confused to me. I wouldn't take her word about the cats. I think this cat is real.'

'How can we tell?'

'I might have something in my panniers.'

'What, bells, books and candles?'

'Christmas dinner.'

'I don't have any electricity. We can't cook Christmas dinner.'

‘We won’t need to cook.’

‘You mean you brought a Chinese takeaway? How will we heat it up?’

‘I didn’t bring a Chinese takeaway.’

Rupert went to rummage in his panniers and a minute later he produced a Fortnum’s luxury hamper.

‘Let’s test the cat,’ he said.

‘I don’t approve of animal testing.’

‘Just this once?’

Rupert opened a small can of something very expensive-looking. Soon they knew the cat was real all right. Unless ghosts were keen on caviar, which Polly rather doubted.

While she unpacked the hamper, Rupert went outside to do his Good King Wenceslas impression. Soon he’d done his Boy Scout stuff as well and had a fire going in the hearth. So they could mull some wine and make some coffee.

‘We’ll sort something out,’ said Rupert, as he polished off the sherry trifle.

‘It must include this cottage and this cat.’

‘It definitely must include the cat.’ Rupert nodded. ‘After all, it led me to this cottage. I saw it prancing down the lane and thought, if I follow the trail of paw prints, maybe I'll meet someone sane, somebody who can help me.'

'So you found the cottage—'

'Yes, and the door was open—'

' And there were all my things inside—'

' And I was very tired—'

' And so you thought you'd have a little rest.'

'I'm still quite sleepy. It's a long drive back to London. I was sort of wondering if I could stay tonight?'

'What do you think, cat?' asked Polly, stroking it between its ears. Yes, now it understood these people were a source of caviar, it cheerfully consented to being stroked. 'Perhaps we ought to let him stay? He brought our dinner, didn't he?'

As Rupert's hand caressed her bump, Polly knew they'd reach a compromise. The cottage could be fixed. Maybe she could bear to live in London at least some of the time? They'd also have a place in Devon for their summer holidays. How great was that?

'We can make it work. Can't we, cat?' she whispered.

'Miaow,' the cat replied.

** The End **

Find out more about Margaret James and her novels

here: https://www.choc-lit.com/productcat/margaret-james/

Margaret's novels include: Girl in Red Velvet, Magic Sometimes Happens, The Wedding Diary, The Penny Bangle, The Golden Chain & *The Silver Locket.*

Beam Me Up, Scotty

Jackie Ladbury

Merry Berry was slowly turning into a block of ice as she stood, waiting, in the market square of her home town. Her pink Christmas fairy dress complete with sparkly wings and matching sparkly gloves were, unsurprisingly, failing to keep out the cold. Her nose was turning red, and if they didn't get going soon she'd be more Rudolph the Reindeer than Christmas Tree Fairy.

The huge Christmas tree that had been trundled into the market square that afternoon loomed over her like a giant nightmare, and her smile, that was always at the ready, dimmed as a rickety wooden platform was hastily rigged up over the top of the tree.

One lone spotlight was to light her up as she flew into the sky, courtesy of a cherry-picker which would set her down on the wooden platform, giving the illusion that she was standing on the tip of the tree – the perfect Christmas fairy. Laser beams would strafe the sky as the Christmas lights were switched on, hopefully to festive cheers and the popping of corks. The publicity she garnered for this act, said Joel, her agent, would be enough to shoot her Christmas song into the charts; she would be famous, and her agent would be quids in.

It was just unfortunate that she was terrified of heights, she thought, shivering more out of fear than the bitter cold of the night as the massive cherry-picker with its long, yellow neck rumbled into the square.

Snow had started to drift down prettily, adding to the magic of Christmas, but within minutes it had become more ostrich feather than duck down, cascading down in a thick torrent, threatening to hide the stage from view. A cutting wind appeared from nowhere, whipping the snowflakes into a whirling dervish, hitting Merry's eyes and landing coldly on her cheeks.

'Five minutes to kick off, love?' Terry the crane driver shouted against the wind as he rattled a bunch of keys indicating that he was ready to fire up the great yellow beast. He squinted up at the wooden platform which swayed from side to side slightly as the wind caught it.

'Do you think it's safe, Terry?' Her voice wobbled infuriatingly, betraying her concern.

Terry, who was on the Christmas Committee said, 'It was approved back in July, so …' He shrugged, shaking his head imperceptibly.

It wasn't really an answer and they both knew it, but she also knew that Joel would insist that it was safe, regardless of the evidence to the contrary. But then, this was the guy who had suggested that she danced on Brighton beach one stormy evening as towering waves crashed around her, just so he could get a fabulous Instagram shot.

As if conjuring him up, he appeared by her side hunched inside a leather coat, his annoying cap set at a jaunty angle. He didn't appear to notice that Merry's whole body shook as Scott the lighting engineer draped a blanket around her shoulders.

She smiled grateful thanks and pulled it tight around her neck.

'I don't think you should be doing this, Merry.' Scott addressed Merry but directed a glare at Joel. 'We should cancel it,' he added. Three sets of eyes looked over at the tree and then up at the sky as snow fell in a sheet of white, threatening to render the whole act useless.

'Nonsense, she'll only be up there for ten minutes, it'll be fine,' Joel replied without missing a beat. 'I'll hold your blanket,' he said firmly, removing Merry's blanket, squashing any fanciful ideas she might have of keeping it with her.

Scott touched Merry's arm. 'Just say the word and I'll put a stop to this.'

Merry smiled gratefully. 'Joel's right, it's only ten minutes and it's just snow.'

'I'll come up with you, then,' Scott said, determination in his voice.

Merry giggled. 'You can't do that, it would ruin the whole point of me being a lone fairy on top of the tree.' She faltered, wistfully wishing the dreamy Scott could wrap his comforting arms around her as she was hoisted up on her solitary perch. 'Anyway, isn't your job to make sure the laser lights roam around the sky while the spotlight is on me?'

Scott sighed. 'Yes, you're right.'

'There you are then,' she said as she bravely stepped into the cage. She locked onto Scott's worried eyes until the snow obliterated the beautiful cornflower-blue of his irises.

Scott hated to see the fear in Merry's eyes; she'd done a sterling job at hiding it, but he knew her well enough. Joel didn't care – he was in it purely for the money and Scott wished he could put him in the cherry-picker and blast him into oblivion.

He desperately wanted to put an end to this piece of madness and wondered who the hell had sanctioned it, but Merry was right; ten minutes tops and she'd be down again, safe and sound, even if he would be holding his breath the whole time.

He needed to focus on his job which was to turn the lasers on and direct the spotlight on her until she was safely down again – and in his arms – he added to himself, knowing that even Father Christmas probably couldn't grant that wish.

He readied his spotlight as Merry rose into the sky, stepped gingerly onto the platform and positioned her microphone. She began to sing, her voice pure and sweet.

As he exhaled a deep sigh of relief, the wind whipped itself into a frenzy and the precarious wooden ledge pitched at an awkward angle. Merry stumbled and grabbed at the thin safety rope that surrounded her, but still she fell and one leg wedged itself in the corner of the ledge, twisting under her bottom.

'Get her down from there,' Scott yelled as his laser light picked up her frightened eyes. He saw a shoe fall as if in slow motion and ran frantically towards it, his arms open wide, fearing that Merry would fall.

Joel gawped and raised his phone into the air, angling it towards the show being acted out in front of him.

'Go and get her, you idiot. Can't you see she's stuck?' Scott bellowed into the wind.

Joel seemed in no particular hurry to save his client as he continued to film her on his phone. He squared up to Scott, a smirk on his face. 'You go and get her, if you're so concerned. Don't think I haven't noticed you ogling her, by the way.'

'You think this is a good time to bring that up?'

Joel, smiled, a gleam of something in his eye as he turned back to his phone, punching in some numbers.

Scott jumped into the cherry-picker stationed behind the tree, but there were no keys and no sign of Terry. Panic set in, and without thinking he began to climb up the neck of the huge crane, desperate to get to Merry before she fell. Snow blinded him, his numb fingers and clumsy feet sliding more times than he could count, but finally he lunged at the tree, caught the top branches and clambered on to the ledge to reach the love of his life. 'I'm here,' he cried, his breath rasping and ragged.

‘My saviour.’ Merry clasped her hands to her breast and then flung them outwards blowing kisses as if thanking her audience.

Scott lifted her up in one easy motion and the crowd went wild. He placed her gently in the cage as he heard the beast rumbling into life: Terry must have returned on hearing the commotion.

They made their way slowly to the ground, Merry’s arms clasped tightly around Scott’s neck, her face nestled perfectly into his chest. Scott smoothed her hair as he raised his eyes heavenward to briefly thank Father Christmas for this unexpected miracle.

He didn’t set her down when they hit solid ground, and she seemed to be in no hurry to be released, the trauma setting up another round of trembling in her delicate body.

Camera phones flashed manically and Joel, grinning, winked at Merry before concentrating on his phone once more. ‘Brilliant job. Trending on Twitter already – interview on Breakfast TV tomorrow morning.’

‘What are you suggesting?’ Merry fluttered her eyelashes coquettishly. She raised her head briefly to give her thrilled audience a wide smile, before returning to the sanctity of Scott’s warm and safe chest, where she intended to stay for a very long time.

** The End **

Find out more about Jackie Ladbury and her novels here: https://www.rubyfiction.com/productcat/jackie-ladbury/

Jackie's novels include: Happy Christmas Eve & The Potter's Daughter.

The Christmas Angel

Marie Laval

Max's breath steamed in the frosty morning as he stuffed the small padded envelope in the pocket of his anorak and locked the narrow boat. He glanced at the name painted on the hull and sniggered once again. *The Jolly Duck.* Could there be a more ridiculous name for a boat belonging to a taciturn six-foot-tall man who only liked his own company and was an expert at discouraging any small talk from fellow boat owners with a single glance of his steely grey eyes?

No, there definitely was nothing jolly about him. *The Grumpy Runaway* or *The Miserable Loner* would suit much better, along with a few other names, all too rude to paint on the side of a canal boat.

His army boots made crunching noises on the icy tow path and the air smelled of snow and coal fires as he walked towards Castleton town centre. Images of cosy homes filled with laughter and love flickered in his mind, and suddenly it was like a fist tightening around his heart and squeezing hard. How would it feel to spend Christmas with people who actually cared – a woman he loved, children even? For years Christmas had been spent in field hospitals or army barracks wherever in the world he happened to be posted, and it had suited him fine. This year, however, he would be alone on his boat, drinking a can of beer or two and eating baked beans on toast and perhaps a couple of supermarket value mince pies …

A pale yellow sun brought no warmth to the frosty landscape. The canal would soon freeze over. He had been lucky to make it to Castleton in time for Christmas.

He felt for the envelope in his pocket again, and the mysterious gift his friend had entrusted him with before he died. As usual when he thought of Ben, sadness and guilt brought a lump to his throat. Memories of the fateful day their ambulance was attacked on the way to a remote Afghan village were as painful and vivid as ever. Ben's injuries had been much worse than his. 'You have to get this to Leila,' Ben had said in a weak voice, gesturing to a small package on the bedside table. 'Promise me you'll give it to my sister at Christmas. Promise me,' Ben had repeated, so Max had promised. That was the last time he'd talked to his friend.

When his contract had come to an end, Max hadn't renewed it. He wanted to be alone, have time and space to think about the future, so he came back to

England, bought the boat and travelled north to Castleton, and to Leila. In a way, keeping Ben's promise had given him a purpose. Who knows what he would have been doing with himself otherwise? And who knows what he'd do once he'd delivered Ben's gift ...

Leila ran a café in Castleton – Leila's Pantry. The town was so small it wasn't hard to find. The bell tinkled as he pushed the door, and he was immediately surrounded by smells of coffee, bacon and warm bread mingling with the fresh scent of pine from the massive Christmas tree near the counter.

'Hi there! I'm Tom.' A young lad greeted him with a smile. 'Would you like a menu?'

Max hesitated. He'd only come to give Leila her present, but the café felt warm and cosy, and he was hungry. He glanced at the menu board and ordered a Full English and some black coffee.

'Will it be a traditional breakfast or a Leila's Special?' the lad asked.

Max frowned. 'What's a Leila's Special?'

'One of those.' Tom pointed to a notice board displaying post-it notes with names of drinks and foods scribbled on.

'Sorry, son, I don't get you.'

‘That’s the Pay It Forward Board,’ the lad explained. ‘You know, when someone settles their bill they pay for something extra. We write what they’ve bought on a note, pin it on there and people who are struggling financially can come and pick something for free.’

Max nodded. ‘That’s a nice idea for Christmas.’

‘It’s not just for Christmas. You’re not from round here, are you? We do this all year round. You see, Leila, the owner, doesn’t want anyone in Castleton to be cold, hungry or lonely if she can help it … So what will it be? Traditional or Leila’s Special Full English?’

‘Traditional for me, son, and I’ll pay for another one to stick on your Pay it Forward Board … by the way, is Leila here? I’m—I was a friend of her brother’s and he gave me a present for her.’

The boy’s eyes widened. ‘You knew Ben? It’s so awful what happened …’

‘Yes, it is.’ He didn’t want to talk about it. Not now. Not ever.

Thankfully, the lad didn’t insist. ‘Leila nipped out but she won’t be long.’

Max sat at an empty table under a blackboard advertising a Christmas Special event – *Order of the day: a good meal and good company, friendship and plenty of Christmas cheer! Everyone welcome. No need to book. There's always room at the inn.*

He sighed. Friends and cheer were in short supply since he'd left the army, and silence and loneliness were the order of *his* days. Christmas day would be no different on the not so jolly *Jolly Duck*.

The lad brought his order over and Max made quick work of the delicious breakfast. He had almost finished when a woman wrapped in a bright red coat walked in. Her cheeks were flushed from the cold, her hair a dark and shiny mass of curls under a white woolly hat. Max's heart missed a beat.

Leila. It had to be her. It wasn't just that she looked a bit like Ben, it was as if his heart, his soul recognised her …

She glanced at him and her lips parted on a gasp, as if she too recognised him. What an idiot he was! Of course she recognised him. Ben must have sent her photos over the years. They'd worked together as army medics for over a decade after all.

He rose to his feet whilst she pulled her woolly hat off and walked towards him. 'You're Max,' she said when she reached him.

He nodded, tongue-tied suddenly.

‘I’ve been expecting you. Ben said you’d be here for Christmas, and here you are. Right on time.’

‘He told you? But how … when …?’ Max asked, finding his voice at last.

‘He called me from the hospital. One of the nurses was holding the phone. It was the last time I spoke to him.’ Her voice wobbled and tears filled her chocolate-brown eyes. ‘He talked so much about you over the years,’ she added, ‘that I feel as if I know you already.’

‘He talked a lot about you too. He was very proud of you,’ Max replied, his throat constricting as Ben’s words danced in his mind. *‘Leila’s an angel ... the kindest woman you can ever meet. She works too hard, like you. I despair of her ever meeting the right man ...’*

Yes, Ben had talked a lot about his little sister … and it seemed everything he’d said about her was true. He hadn’t mentioned, however, that she had the most beautiful smile and the deepest brown eyes.

Leila let out a sob and wiped her eyes. ‘Oh dear … I promised myself I wouldn’t get all weepy and emotional when I finally met you, and look at me now.’

‘Don’t worry about it.’ Feeling embarrassingly weepy and emotional himself, he looked away and pulled a chair out for her.

‘This is for you,’ he said as he handed her the envelope.

She took it with trembling fingers and clutched it to her heart. ‘Thank you. It means a lot to have Ben’s last ever Christmas present.’

‘I’m sorry it took so long, but I’ve been travelling on my canal boat and it’s not very fast.’

‘You live on a boat? How lovely! How do you find it?’

‘It’s quiet.’ It was lonely too, but he enjoyed it, most of the time.

‘It must be wonderful to cruise around, choose where you stop for the night and move on when you want to. I’d love to go on a trip up and down the canal one day.’

‘I’ll take you, if you like,’ he offered without thinking. He immediately cursed his stupidity. What was he saying? He had no plans to stay in Castleton. What’s more, a woman like Leila would never want to spend time with him. The cosy atmosphere of the café and the woman’s smile and thoughtful brown eyes must be getting to him.

To his surprise, she gave him a beaming smile. 'What a great idea! I'd love to. Perhaps on Boxing Day if you're free?' She fiddled with the envelope. 'Every year Ben sent me ornaments for my Christmas tree from wherever he was in the world. I wonder what it is this time.'

Max frowned. He'd assumed what was in the envelope was important, some jewellery perhaps, but maybe it was only a Christmas ornament. He felt a bit deflated suddenly.

Leila opened the envelope and pulled out a small, bright blue carved figure. She held it in front of her, a look of wonder on her face. 'It's an angel made of like lapis lazuli, and it's far too beautiful to hang on the tree. I'll make a pendant out of it …' She looked at him and smiled. 'I can't thank you enough for bringing me my Christmas angel. It's probably the last thing Ben ever bought.' She started putting the figure back in the envelope but then she suddenly frowned. 'What's this?' She pulled out a piece of paper and Max recognised Ben's handwriting. Her cheeks coloured as she read the message.

'Is everything all right?' he asked, curious.

She nodded and put the message back in the envelope. 'Yes. It was only Ben reminding me to grab every opportunity to have fun … and talking about fun, do you have any plans for tomorrow? If not, you are very welcome to attend our Christmas event here.'

His first instinct was to refuse. Party games, crackers and paper hats weren't his thing. What's more, he didn't know anybody in Castleton and would feel even more like an outsider than usual.

Leila must have sensed his reluctance because she leant over the table. 'You would do me a favour, actually. I'm terribly short-staffed and I could do with a hand.'

Her eyes were like smooth chocolate, and her lips so pink and enticing his resolve faltered. After all, what else did he have to do with his Christmas day? 'Sure. Why not?'

She reclined against the back of her chair and let out a sigh of relief. 'Of course all your drinks and meals will be on the house.'

'There's no need. I'm glad I can help.'

She gave him another dazzling smile. 'Thank you. I'm afraid I have to leave you for now. Too many things to prepare for tomorrow, and like I said, I'm short staffed.'

'Can I help?' Once again, the question had shot out.

She arched her eyebrows. 'Well, now you're asking … how are you with peeling carrots, potatoes and sprouts?'

He arched his eyebrows. 'I'm a devil with a knife. I used to be a surgeon, after all.'

That was a pretty poor joke, but it was his first in months, and for some reason it made her smile.

'In that case, you're hired!'

He spent the rest of the day in the kitchen, preparing vegetables for the Christmas lunch and wrapping sets of cutlery into festive paper napkins as Leila walked in and out, bringing him food and coffee, and her wonderful smile. Tom came in to help too, and chatted about his family, about school and his aspirations for the future. He asked lots of questions about the army, about Max's job, and about Ben, and this time Max didn't mind talking about the past – at least the good bits.

He felt more alive that day than any time during the previous few months. It was the weirdest thing – the feeling of fitting in, of having come home, at last.

When the café closed for the evening, Tom went home and Leila popped her head in the doorway. She looked at the tidy kitchen, with the pots and pans filled with vegetables ready to be steamed or roasted the following morning, the piles of sparkling plates and the carefully wrapped cutlery sets.

'It's a miracle. Thanks to you, everything is ready for tomorrow.'

Could he tell her? Would she understand or would she think he was crazy? Perhaps it was time to be brave.

He took a deep breath. 'I'm the one who needs to thank you. I know we've only just met, but it's like I've known you forever … and …' He stumbled on the last words. Could he tell her that he wanted to stay, to hold her hand, talk to her until the end of the night, and kiss her?

She stepped closer and tilted her face up. 'I feel the same. It's crazy, isn't it? But I think Ben knew it would happen, that's why he sent you. He even wrote on the message that he was being cupid.'

As he walked back to the boat late that evening, having seen Leila home to her small flat above the café and shared a tasty curry and a bottle of wine, he looked at the stars and said a thousand thanks to his friend. Thanks to Ben, there would be no more running away. No more brooding, silence or loneliness.

And he would change the boat's name to *Christmas Angel*. After all, it had brought him luck. And Leila.

** The End **

Find out more about Marie Laval and her novels here: https://www.choc-lit.com/productcat/marie-laval/

Marie's novels include: Escape to the Little Chateau, Bluebell's Christmas Magic, A Paris Fairy Tale & Little Pink Taxi.

New Beginnings
Sue McDonagh

The Tax and MOT renewal arrived for their VW campervan in the same post, addressed to Jack.

She pulled her coat and woolly hat on, slid open the orange side door and climbed in.

'Hi, Jack!'

'I've put Dad in the camper,' her son had said. 'He's not very happy, 'cause he can't see over the steering wheel.' They'd laughed together, and she'd waved him off with a smile before she let the tears fall.

'Bloody freezing in here. I thought you were taking me to France?' Jack berated her from his purple urn, about the same size as an old-fashioned sweetie jar.

'I thought it was you taking me!'

More green than orange, these days, the van, what with the rain, which clashed hideously with the patchwork curtains and cushions she'd fed through the old sewing machine, while Jack arranged the engine in bits across the garage floor. Seeing it now, he would have had a heart attack. If he hadn't already had one.

They'd never used it, after all Jack's plans for their retirement in the sun. Her son started it up every week, while she pretended to be busy in the kitchen.

The dog had followed her out and hopped onto the passenger seat, staring loftily about him. Her two favourite boys, in the front seat of the van. And she was the passenger.

'Where you off to, Nan?' Her pink-cheeked and glossy granddaughter, Charlie, sprang alongside to investigate the cupboards. She lifted out orange mugs and examined them with a critical eye. 'These are so cool! Mum and Dad are working late tonight, remember? Can we get fish and chips and eat them by the sea? I could take photos and put them on Instagram.' Charlie crooked her index fingers. 'Cross Generational Lifestyle!' Head cocked, she added, 'We'd need a tablecloth. And a whistling kettle. Have you got a kettle?' She whooped as the lime-green kettle was produced from another cupboard.

'Your dad thinks I should sell it.'

'The kettle?' Charlie laughed.

'The van, silly.'

'Do you want to?'

'I – don't know if I can–'

'Drive it?'

‘I’m perfectly capable of driving it!’

‘What then?’ She shrugged her sharp shoulders. ‘It needs a clean … What else?’

It was always so simple for the young.

‘It’s too cold for the beach,’ she tried. ‘And I don’t even know if there’s any gas to boil the kettle … or water, come to that.’

Charlie sucked her teeth. ‘Sisterrr,’ she said with attitude. ‘Who is it who tells me to put on a jumper when I want the heating on? We’ll bring blankets! Come onnnn! We can drink coke! Or you can take a flask of that old lady tea you like.’

‘She’s so cool,’ said Jack, impressed. ‘Off you go then.’

‘You go collect some blankets, Charlie. I’ll get my bag.’ She dawdled behind her granddaughter a moment, stomach in free-fall, then lifted Jack up and stowed him behind the bed.

‘Sorry, lovely. My turn to drive now.’

** The End **

Find out more about Sue McDonagh and her novels here:

https://www.choc-lit.com/productcat/sue-mcdonagh/

Sue’s novels include: Escape to the Art Café, Meet Me at the Art Café & Summer at the Art Café.

A Christmas Cake Wish

Hannah Pearl

Nat King Cole's voice crooned softly, wishing them a merry Christmas. Outside a chill wind ruffled the trees, but inside the cottage the ancient Aga kept them toasty. The old pine table held platters of golden roast potatoes, peas and carrots, and the obligatory dish of sprouts, but they were small bowls as they only needed to serve two.

'Can I pass you another Yorkshire pudding, Nanna?'

'Thanks, Holly. These aren't bad for frozen ones.' Her nan took another bite and nodded approvingly. 'Not bad at all.'

Holly was relieved that her gran hadn't minded her making a few small changes to make their Christmas dinner a bit easier to prepare. Nanna had still insisted on doing most of it herself. 'Gravy?' This, too, was instant, made from granules. Nanna had been worried about how they'd make it when they weren't having turkey and had been greatly reassured that Holly had a plan. 'Are you sure you're happy with your nut roast?' Holly asked.

‘It’s much better than dry turkey. Don’t you worry about me, love. If this is what you were having, then it’s fine for me too.’ Nanna picked up her knife and fork and began to tuck in. ‘The only thing I miss,’ she said, as she cleared her plate, ‘is having the wish bone to fight over. Me and my brothers were terrors for who got to pull it. My wishes always came true when I got a turn, so I wasn’t afraid to resort to fisticuffs to try to win. We turned my poor mother’s hair grey, I’m sure.’

Holly smiled.

Nanna continued, ‘I’m only sorry we’re such a small family these days. Still, we’ve got each other, don’t we? Now, I made this so let’s see if this works just as well.’ Nanna pulled a contraption from her pocket. It appeared to be two match sticks held together with masking tape. ‘It’s a vegetarian wishbone. Now, grab one end and pull. Whoever gets the knobble of tape at the top gets their wish.’

Holly closed her eyes. What she really wanted right now was a glass of wine or a seasonal glass of brandy or port, but her gran had never been a big drinker and rarely had alcohol in the house.

‘Well done, Holly, love. I hope you wished for something special. You deserve it.’ Nanna reached across and took her hand. It was lucky that you weren't supposed to say your wishes out loud, because Holly felt guilty for not thinking of something more selfless.

Goodness knew something needed to change soon to make Nanna's life easier. Her gran was finding the stairs increasingly tricky and the cottage had been more dusty than Holly had ever seen it at her last visit. Though, now she came to look again, the walls were pristine. Had they had a new coat of paint? Holly looked around as her gran moved bowls and carried a large cake to the table.

'Nanna, that's enormous! How are we going to eat all of that?'

'I've invited Joe from next door to come and share it. He's been helping me in the house a bit recently. He's ever so nice.' Holly could have sworn that her nan blushed as she spoke.

'Your new neighbour?' Holly had visions of an old man, also in his eighties, visiting for tea and cake. *Good*. Her nan deserved not to be lonely anymore. Not that Holly could remember the last time she'd had a hug from anyone except Nanna either.

'Now, make a wish when we cut it. If you find the silver sixpence it might come true,' Nanna said. This time Holly didn't hold back and wished for someone who would give her the kind of hugs she missed, with strong arms which left you knowing you were safe. She took a bite of cake and waved her hand in front of her mouth.

'How much booze did you put in here, Nanna?'

'A bit,' the old lady admitted. 'I figured we'd need it, not that I wanted a bottle on the table or anything, so I've been feeding the cake brandy for weeks. Is it strong?'

'I reckon I'll be merry when I finish this. I might sleep on the sofa if that's okay and drive home tomorrow.'

'Why don't you stay here … permanently, I mean. I've been thinking, I've found a nice one-bedroom apartment in the retirement complex in the village, no stairs.'

'Nanna, you don't have to move out. I'm fine where I am.'

'You had mice there last week, and I know there's mould behind the door that you didn't want me to see. No, I've been to the solicitor and I've got the ball rolling. This place was always going to be yours one day. Might as well happen when I still get to enjoy seeing you living here. Besides, Vera's ever so lonely since she lost Ted. This way I can join her for bingo twice a week. We were thinking of starting a knitting club, too. Apparently, there's one in the village; they meet in the pub on a Saturday lunchtime. "Stitch and Bitch" it's called. We won't be bitching, but I like the idea of crafting together. I could give crochet lessons and Vera could teach us about her wonderful baking. We could call it "Hooking and Cooking".'

Holly spluttered on her tea. 'Nanna!'

Her gran laughed, clearly delighted with her own joke. '"Knit and Knatter" it is then. Bit boring if you ask me, but we won't offend anyone, I guess – apart from Mabel, but she's offended by everything these days.' The doorbell rang. 'That'll be Joe.' Nanna patted her hair to make sure it was in place.

Holly grinned and took another bite of the boozy cake, all the better to fortify herself before meeting her gran's new friend. The currants were plump and juicy and the icing just the right thickness to be sweet but not overpowering. She chewed but something caught the back of her throat and she began to cough. A moment later, strong arms wrapped her from behind and began to squeeze. She tapped them to show she was alright, reached for a napkin and spat the silver sixpence into it.

'Ooh, hope you wished for something lovely,' Nanna said.

'Not to choke to death on the cake would probably have been a good one.' Holly wiped her mouth then looked up and found that the arms which had been about to give her the Heimlich belonged to a young man, about her age, with golden hair and green eyes.

'This is Joe,' Nanna said, grinning. 'He's been helping me since he moved in. Looks like he doesn't mind helping you too. He's ever so strong.'

Holly blushed as red as Rudolph's nose. Nearly scarlet enough, in fact, to match the fluffy Santa-style jumper that her new neighbour was wearing.

'Tea, Joe?' Nanna offered.

'Thanks. My sisters opened the Baileys about three hours ago and I could do with something refreshing.'

'I'll pop the kettle on. Why don't you take Holly out to the shed and show her what we've been planning?'

"Shed" was a misnomer. Nanna's house and her neighbour's had long thin gardens, separated by a low wooden fence. At the bottom, against the back wall, a brick building spanned the width of both. 'Your Nanna saw me fixing the roof and asked if I'd patch up her side too,' Joe explained.

‘Are you a builder?’

‘Carpenter, but I’m pretty handy. I had help from a mate in the trade to run the electrics out here, but I patched up the walls and laid the floor myself.’ He opened the door and switched on a light. What had previously been a dark, dank tumbledown room, filled with a pile of old lawn mowers and broken bikes, was now a clean, bright work space. A beautiful oak counter ran against the length of the room. Holly ran her fingers over it. A matching chair with red cushions covered in holly print called for her to sit and make herself comfy. ‘Your nan said you make jewellery in your spare time. She had me build these shelves to hold your supplies.’ Joe pointed to a display behind her. His simple description didn’t do justice to the ornately crafted wood, with all of the edges rounded and more holly leaves carved into the sides. Boxes held pliers and beads, silver wire and colourful glass. ‘Your nan told me about her plans to move last week. This is from me, to welcome you to the cottage.’ Joe reached to the top shelf and lifted down a small box.

Holly lifted the lid. It was a jewellery box made from the same wood as the counter but polished until the grain shone. Inside, it was lined with fabric to match her cushions. Joe reached past and turned a tiny handle at the back to wind it. A ballerina turned and a small music box played 'The Holly and the Ivy'.

Holly reached into her handbag and pulled out a small velvet pouch. She opened it and showed Joe the necklace she had finished that morning. A silver star pendant hung from a chain. The inside was filled with glass, inset with metal, which caught the light and glittered.

'It's like a shooting star, you should make a wish,' Joe told her, clearly as awed by her skills as she had been by his. He took the necklace from her and fastened it around her neck. 'Beautiful.' *Was he talking about the pendant or her?* Probably best not to ask, she decided, just in case she ended up disappointed again.

In the distance, Holly heard a glass smash and the chatter of voices that had carried on the wind fell silent. A moment later laughter sounded and a cork popped. Holly found herself wishing that one day she would have a big family to share special days with too.

'Sorry about the noise,' Joe said. 'They'll be gone tomorrow.' But he grinned as he said it, and Holly immediately knew he'd miss them when they went.

'You have a big family?'

‘I’m one of five and all of the others have three kids each already, so when they voted on the venue for this year, they ganged up and I didn’t stand a chance of having it anywhere else. I’m glad they’re happy, but I think I’ll be cleaning up until new year.’

‘And replacing broken glasses by the sounds of things.’

‘It’s all part of the fun when you’ve got a house full of kids. Let’s lock up and get back to your gran. I promised her I’d stay for some cake.’

Holly opened the door to leave and stopped. Joe bumped into her. She nudged him back into the studio. ‘Wait here a sec, my nanna is playing tricks on me.’

She stepped back outside and stared up at the mistletoe that hung from the studio door. It hadn’t been there when they went in, and she wondered how on earth Nanna had climbed up to fix it there, but she needed to move it before Joe saw and things got awkward. She was thinking about using her new chair to climb up, when the door opened again and Joe came out and noticed what she was looking at.

‘We don’t have to use it,’ she told him, not managing to meet his eyes with her own.

‘But if we want to … may I?’

She nodded. She closed her eyes and felt his lips softly touch her own.

'That star must be magic,' he told her. 'It looks like my dream did come true after all.'

** The End **

Find out more about Hannah Pearl and her novels here: https://www.rubyfiction.com/productcat/hannah-pearl/

Hannah's novels include: Daisy's Summer Mission, Daisy's Christmas Gift Shop, Burn, It's My Birthday & Evie's Little Black Book.

The Bookshop on the Corner

Berni Stevens

Zach grinned to himself as he glanced at the distinct lack of messages on his phone. Three weeks off work now until the North American part of the tour kicked off in the New Year. Three weeks without having to listen to a certain keyboard player ranting on about the discarded track (which he'd written) and wanted reinstated on the tour play list. Three weeks of peace. Well, relative peace anyway.

Christmas mayhem was in full swing, and it seemed everybody suddenly wanted a piece of Zach over the holidays. The temptation was to pull up the drawbridge, so to speak, and stay put in his own place. He really didn't fancy spending Christmas shuttling around the M25 in dreary circles, or sitting in a traffic jam on said motorway until January. Very, very boring. Then there'd be the inevitable, "Why don't you settle down with a nice girl?" or "When are you going to get a proper job?" conversations.

If only they all realised his present job earned him more than enough to pay for a pretty nice flat in Finchley, and get him a cool car too. Wouldn't they find that surprising? "Playing around with those musician types," his mother called the only profession he'd ever been interested in. Or good at. Zach smiled to himself. His smile faded as he thought about the unavoidable Christmas shopping. His two nieces and three nephews were the biggest headache. What did he know about a five-year-old girl and her seven-year-old sister? Only that they were usually covered in mud (and worse), from spending a lot of time around horses and in stables, so dolls really weren't an option and would be exceedingly unwelcome. Books? He couldn't really visualise them sitting still long enough to read even two words, but perhaps they read at bedtime? Or were read to? He sighed. Well this wouldn't get him anywhere. He decided to have a look around the local shops for inspiration. If that failed, he'd resort to internet shopping. He shrugged into his warm overcoat. Now what was the name of that bookshop his friend Seth had told him about?

The cold air snapped at him with its icy jaws the moment he stepped outside the flat. He felt sorely tempted to hurtle back inside, shut the door and order in a takeaway.

'You're made of sterner stuff than that, Zach, old buddy,' he told himself, and headed off towards the shops.

He spotted the children's bookshop on the corner, and it seemed almost to beckon to him. Its windows shone with a cosy, welcoming glow, which blazed out across the pavement. It couldn't be all bad, could it? With his head down against the biting wind, he didn't see the small brunette until they collided by the door of the shop.

'So sorry,' she muttered. 'Oh … hey, Zach, fancy seeing you here.'

'Sorry …?' Zach peered down. 'Oh, Anna, hi. You shopping too?'

'No, this is where I buy all my intellectual reading.' She laughed.

Zach held the door open for her, and she went in the shop ahead of him.

He looked around at the shelves of brightly coloured books stacked from floor to ceiling and blew out a frustrated breath. 'Where on earth do I start …?'

Anna smiled sympathetically. 'With the age of the child.'

Zach could see why she was the linchpin of the band, and Seth's "go to" person for most things. She ran the PR for the band – it appeared – effortlessly, and yet she still managed a smile for everyone. He wondered how he'd never really noticed how lovely her smile was before. They'd been working together for years, the three of them. Her hair was gorgeous too, so shiny … he gave himself a mental shake.

'Five of 'em. Two girls, three boys – although the girls might as well be boys.'

Anna laughed. 'Tomboys, huh?'

'Horse mad. The boys are a bit older and all into superheroes.'

Anna was already over by a section in the far corner, efficiently pulling out books and laying them on a nearby table. 'How old are the girls?' She deftly flicked through a picture book and set it back on the table.

'Five and seven.'

She frowned slightly and whittled the pile down by three books. 'Have a peek at those.'

Zach looked at her in amazement. 'Were you ever a librarian?'

She laughed. 'Definitely not, but I do love books.'

He looked at the books she'd picked. Beautiful picture books, with illustrated pony stories. Before he could even blink, she'd added matching pony models, complete with saddles and bridles.

'Different-coloured ponies and different stories, so they can read each other's stories, but tell their own pony apart from the other – so no arguments.' She looked up at him and grinned, her dark eyes sparkling. 'How old are the boys?'

Not only gorgeous but clever too.

'Ermmm … seven, eight and ten.' He really hoped that was right.

Anna went back to the shelves and soon selected a collection of superhero books, picture books for the two youngest and a more adult-looking book for the ten-year-old.

'You might want to get the older boy a model of Wolfman or something,' she suggested. 'Not suitable for the younger ones, of course.'

'You're amazing.' Zach ran a hand through his wiry ginger hair, making it stand up on end. 'I've always known you were amazing of course, but I've never really just stood still long enough to witness you actually being … amazing.'

She flushed with pleasure. 'You can buy me a drink to say thanks.'

'To hell with a drink, I'm buying you dinner.'

'It's a deal. Go buy books and ponies.' She pointed to the cash desk.

Anna watched Zach walk over to the cash desk with his arms full of books and ponies. After all the years they'd worked together, he'd never seemed to notice her, not as a woman anyway. She'd always been efficient, reliable Anna. Actually, she was usually manically busy Anna. She'd watched him drift in and out of occasional relationships and, to be honest, had drifted in and out of a few herself, too. But for her, it had always been Zach. His innate kindness to everyone, and his loyalty to the band, told her he was a good bloke. She knew Seth would never have stayed mates with him for so long if he hadn't trusted him completely. She owed him a big "thank you" for telling her he'd recommended this bookshop to Zach. Although she would never tell him how she'd staked the shop out for several days in a row. She could almost hear him laughing.

Zach turned at that moment to wave an enormous Christmas bag of goodies at her. 'Where do you fancy going to eat?'

Anywhere with Zach sounded perfect to her.

** The End **

Find out more about Berni Stevens and her novels here:

https://www.choc-lit.com/productcat/berni-stevens/

Berni's novels include: Izzy's Christmas Star, One Magical Christmas, Revenge is Sweet & Dance until Dawn.

A Christmas with a Difference

Evonne Wareham

As soon as he saw her, he knew she was going to cause him trouble.

Just his type, and then some.

He was fine with pulling the Christmas Day shift in the hotel bar, working while everyone else was partying. Really he was. The guests were enjoying themselves and the pay, and the tips, were good. He just didn't need a blonde pixie, with a smile that could power a street full of fairy lights, messing with his mind.

Hmm, are you sure that's all she's messing with?

She'd staked out a table in the corner, with one of the high-backed chairs – the comfiest in the place, naturally – and spread her possessions around her as if she was circling the wagons. Coat, hat, scarf, gloves – everything it took to keep the winter chill away – piled on the chair next to her. Enormous leather bag dumped on another.

And, oh God, his mouth went dry and he swallowed hard. She had her feet up on one of the padded stools. Feet and legs. Under an oversized sweater, with a cross-eyed reindeer on the front, she wore boots.

Boots with thin pencil heels that could skewer a man's heart in the blink of an eye. And legs that went on forever, encased, all the way up to the knee and beyond, in black suede.

He turned away, trying to erase the image from his mind and concentrate on serving a family who had come in for cocktails before their Christmas dinner. He served the drinks, wiped down the bar, and then …

He really couldn't put it off any longer.

Summoning up every ounce of acting skill he could muster – hell, this was Oscar class – he strolled over to her.

'Can I get you something, madam?'

She was looking him up and down. Head to foot. He could feel the heat rising in his face. And that wasn't the only place.

'Oh! That would be nice …' She was staring at his chest. *Name tag. She's looking at your name tag*. The name tag that some bright spark in the kitchen had seen fit to decorate with a tipsy looking glittery Santa that would not come unstuck. He'd tried. Several times. Now Santa was not quite upright and looked even more tipsy. She was grinning. 'Thank you, Scott. I'll have a pot of tea. To start with.'

He got the tea. And, of course, he couldn't just put it down and leave, as he would if it had been a cappuccino or a latte. He had to unload the tray. Pot, cup and saucer, milk jug, sugar bowl. She actually brushed her fingers across his knee, batting her eyelashes and thanking him for the "attention".

The bar was comfortably busy, with parties of guests coming in for drinks before their turkey and plum pudding, and a scattering of couples and singles ordering bar meals instead of the full restaurant blow out. Then those who had chosen to eat in the restaurant early began to drift back, looking for coffee and liqueurs.

The lights on the two Christmas trees twinkled, carols played softly over the speakers, conversation ebbed and flowed and glasses clinked. And all the time he was aware of her, sitting in her corner. She had a tablet on her lap and appeared to be working. She had a toasted sandwich for her lunch – mozzarella, tomato and basil – followed by a very large ice-cream sundae and another pot of tea. His fellow barman, Pete, had come on shift at noon to help out for a couple of hours, but somehow it was never Pete's eye she caught when she wanted vinegar for her side order of fries, or more milk for her tea.

Sometime around three, when the coffee and liqueurs traffic was really heating up, the boss stuck his head in the door and gave her a hard stare, before disappearing again. Scott had his hands full with a production line of Brandy Alexanders – an old-style cocktail that was rich and festive with cream and nutmeg. As soon as he'd made one and everyone at the bar saw it, they all wanted one, plus he had to re-organise the TV to show the Queen's speech, so he lost track for a while.

And then, when he breathed again and looked up, she was gone.

For a second his heart plummeted, but then he saw her. Sitting almost next to him on one of the high stools at the bar, one pink-tipped finger to her rosy mouth as she studied the cocktail menu.

How the hell did she get there?

And if she asks for a Slow Comfortable Screw, I'm going to lose it completely.

She dropped the menu and looked up at him with her evil pixie grin that had been tormenting him for hours. 'When does your shift end?'

'In one minute.' Scott was already stripping off the barman bow tie and name tag and reaching for the leather jacket stashed under the counter.

'Then I'd better settle my bill.'

'All done.' He had the jacket. He was not going to answer that grin. 'When we agreed that we'd both work over Christmas for the money to go skiing, nothing was said about you planning to work here.'

'Grumpy.' She slid off the stool, teetering on her high heels as he ducked through the pass door and came to stand beside her. She put up a hand to pat his cheek. 'Be a good boy and take your wife home. I'm waiting for my Christmas present.'

'What makes you think I got you one?' he growled.

'Because you're a complete sweetie and I love you.' She leaned forward and the sparkle in her eyes melted everything inside him, before her smile turned totally wicked. 'I can't wait to give you yours.' She stepped closer to whisper in his ear. 'If you're really good, I'll leave the boots on.'

** The End **

Find out more about Evonne Wareham and her novels here: https://www.choc-lit.com/productcat/evonne-wareham/

Evonne's novels include: A Wedding on the

Riviera, What Happens at Christmas, Summer in San Remo, Out of Sight Out of Mind & Never Coming Home.

Introducing Choc Lit Publishing

We're an independent publisher creating
a selection of quality fiction.
We have two brands:
Choc Lit - w*here heroes are like chocolate – irresistible!*
Romance novels which includes the heroes point of view.
Ruby Fiction - *stories that inspire emotions!*
Women's fiction, romance and thrillers.
See our selection here:
www.choc-lit.com & **www.rubyfiction.com**
We'd love to hear how you enjoyed *Cosy Christmas Treats*. Please leave a review where you purchased the novel or visit **www.choc-lit.com** and give your feedback.
Choc Lit & Ruby novels are selected by genuine readers like yourself. We only publish stories our Tasting Panel want to see in print. Our reviews and awards speak for themselves.
Could you be a Star Selector and join our Tasting Panel?
Would you like to play a role in choosing which novels we decide to publish? Do you enjoy reading women's fiction, romance and thrillers? Then you could be perfect for our Tasting Panel.
See here: **www.choc-lit.com/join-the-choc-lit-tasting-panel**
Keep in touch:
Sign up for our weekly newsletter for all the latest news and offers:www.spread.choc-lit.com.
Follow us on
Twitter: @ChocLituk
Facebook: Choc Lit
Instagram: @choclituk

Printed in Great Britain
by Amazon

54587269R00147